THE SECRET LEMONADE DRINKER
MEETS THE PRESS:

'A promising light comedy from a budding Leslie Thomas.'
Sunday Telegraph

'A vulgarian's delight, a swift-moving anthology of
wonderfully funny and releasing all-male jokes of a splendid
crudity, a lavatory wall of a book . . . a first novel by a
considerable humorist.'
New Fiction

'Not many books make me laugh out loud on the
underground, but Guy Bellamy's did. I haven't laughed
so much since Lucky Jim.'
Hampstead and Highgate Express

'A sexual comedy, parts of which could perhaps be read
as a serious commentary on the way we live now, and all
of it as a wry look at the longevity of the double standard.'
The Guardian

'I shall remember this book for its dialogue: just as his
characters are potent beyond the norm, so also are they
witty . . . great fun.'
Northern Echo

The Secret Lemonade Drinker

Guy Bellamy

CORGI BOOKS
A DIVISION OF TRANSWORLD PUBLISHERS LTD

THE SECRET LEMONADE DRINKER
A CORGI BOOK 0 552 10796 4

Originally published in Great Britain
by Martin Secker & Warburg Ltd.

PRINTING HISTORY

Secker & Warburg edition published 1977
Corgi edition published 1978
Corgi edition reprinted 1978

This book is set in Plantin 10/10½ pt. solid.

Corgi Books are published by Transworld Publishers Ltd.,
Century House, 61–63 Uxbridge Road, Ealing, London, W5 5SA

Made and printed in Great Britain by
Richard Clay (The Chaucer Press), Ltd., Bungay, Suffolk

FOR MY MOTHER

At the end of one millenium and nine centuries of Christianity, it remains an unshakable assumption of the law in all Christian countries and of the moral judgment of Christians everywhere, that if a man and a woman entering a room together close the door behind them, the man will come out sadder, and the woman wiser.

H.L.MENCKEN

What we are witnessing is the triumph of the clitoral after three thousand years of phallic hegemony.

HENRY BECH

ONE

There is nothing like marriage for removing a man's carnal desires, he thought, and now it doesn't matter. He took out cigarette number thirty-eight but discovered to his relief that he had no matches. The hiss of the tyres on the road outside told him that the rain had finally started, but on a day like this a rainstorm, an earthquake, a nuclear explosion in the room next door could hardly scratch the black surface of his mood. He went out of his office to look at the business.

The day was nearly over and only one customer remained in the shop, a tall dark-haired girl in jeans and a yellow T-shirt which asked across both breasts and all the way down to her navel: HOW CAN WE LOSE WHEN WE'RE SO SINCERE? He looked at the girl but she was staring back at him, so he turned away to the third spin drier where her colourful underwear was turning and dropping.

Even now he could still be soothed by the swirling activity of a spin drier: it was a kind of television to his bored mind. If the grinning face of the latest show-business-freak had emerged through the knickers to recommend an exciting new brand of cornflakes he would scarcely have been surprised.

He went back into his office to fetch some refills for the Super Brite detergent dispenser on the wall. The Quik Brite dry bleach supply was getting low and he filled that up, too. The cigarette was back in his mouth, but his matchbox was still empty. He opened the drawers of his desk, convinced that there must be a light somewhere, but he was wrong. Weakening as usual, he went out to the girl in the T-shirt. She was probably an art student, he decided. Everybody around here was an art student.

'Have you got a light?' he asked.

'Sure,' she said, and handed him a Zippo. She was a pretty girl but she had depressed him already with only one word—he had once wasted valuable years teaching children English before he realised that an entire generation had already decided to speak American. He lit his cigarette but did not offer her one. It could give her ideas. She was smiling at him in a way that he had once taken to mean that a girl was available.

'Are you waiting to close?' she asked.

He inhaled deeply and imagined the lungs turning from pink to grey and from grey to black.

'No hurry at all,' he said, and walked over to the door. The Christmas lights were twinkling in the street, and in the small market square a twenty-foot Christmas tree was keeping the rain off a tiny crib. Tomorrow the carol-singers would gather around it and money-boxes would be shaken in front of evasive faces. For himself, believing in neither Father Christmas nor God, he found that the holiday wrong-footed him every year.

The antidote to it all lay in a small establishment across the square from his shop. It was called the Coach and Horses although that was not how the customers arrived any more. Locally it was known as the Planet of the Apes because of the long hair and unkempt appearance of its predominantly art student clientele. The Planet was where you could buy happiness in a bottle, and it was where he would be any minute now.

He fetched the keys and the cash-box from his office and collected the money from each machine. The girl in the T-shirt was putting her newly dried clothes into a Sainsbury's paper carrier. He found the way that her chest filled her shirt distracting. He watched her leave and then took the money from the spin drier that she had been using and put the whole lot in the safe in his office.

He looked in the mirror to make sure that he was not about to launch himself into the exciting night life of the Planet with two and half pounds of gunge stacked up in the corner of one eyeball. He could have had that girl, he realised, but he was married and he was thirty-two and he wanted a drink. The face that looked back at him from the mirror seemed a lot older than thirty-two and yet two years ago, when he had married, he looked a lot younger than his age. There was a moral there somewhere. He combed his hair forward, removing the parting that was trying not only to assert itself, but to widen with every month that passed, and wondered whether he should go home now to talk things over with Caroline. But she would be working until midnight, and he wanted a drink.

Drink first, talk later. There was nothing like marriage for concentrating a man's mind on the things that really mattered.

The world's worries were left at the door of the Planet; you picked them up on your way out. Bobby Booth, wearing the same thick sweater and jeans now that he would in June, walked quickly through the rain, head down, hands in pockets, and pushed the door open with his scuffed suede shoes. There were seventy-two minutes of drinking time left, not counting the illegal drinking minutes that might emerge at closing time if the landlord decided to lock the doors and have a late session with the chosen few after the rest of his customers had lurched off into the rain.

The Planet was a small, snug public house with a horseshoe-shaped counter in the middle of the room, and cubicles around the edge in each of which four people could sit in some privacy. Tonight there was also a log fire blazing, and Christmas decorations hanging like cobwebs from the ceiling. As usual, the place was crowded.

But it was still easy enough to see Roland, standing behind a five-inch Havana cigar at the bar and entertaining his usual willing audience.

'Great news, old fruit,' he shouted as Bobby approached. 'I'm in the last eight of the world celibacy championships. Meet the Pope in the quarter finals.'

'Bad as that, is it?' Bobby said. 'I'll have a large Bells, no ice.'

'Bad? My sex life is a disaster area. Probably qualifies for a government grant if only I knew which form to fill in. I'm wondering whether to make a virtue out of necessity and become a monk.'

He handed Bobby a large whisky and bought himself one. He was a big man, a fat man who at the age of thirty-five weighed nearly eighteen stone. His admission of sexual deprivation was unusual: for years he had given the impression

9

that women were forever interrupting his majestic progress through life with propositions of a private nature. He finished his old pint and started his new whisky.

'I think we can declare Christmas open tonight,' he said. 'There will be parties galore. I shall meet a lovely lady and something beautiful will happen to me.'

Bobby drank half his whisky and reluctantly accepted a cigarette. Number thirty-nine.

'What happened to the apostle of bachelorhood then?' he asked. 'Don't buy a book when there's a library? Why should I eat in the same restaurant every night? Remember all that stuff? You gave me to believe that a wild horde of depraved women were after your body.'

Roland looked baffled. 'They were. Now they're not. Funny that.'

He stubbed his cigar out in a large china ashtray on the counter which was immediately cleaned by the landlord, a tall thin man in glasses called Basil, who kept his ashtrays so clean that it seemed only helpful occasionally to drop your ash on the floor.

'What happened to the last girl I saw you with? Carol? Or Karen, or Carrie or whatever her name was? The travel courier bird.'

Roland shook his head. 'She's moved in with a Spanish waiter. Can you imagine? She spent last summer in Spain and got mad about Spaniards. One whiff of a Catalan armpit and her knickers are flying through the air like cushions at a bull-fight.'

The memory of his recently lost lady seemed to subdue him. He retreated into private thoughts about the romance that had died.

'She was a virgin nymphomaniac, you know,' he said eventually.

'A virgin nymphomaniac?'

'I mean, first she was a virgin and then she was a nymphomaniac. The first time I had her was standing up in the car park at the Barley Mow. It was like introducing a bee to honey.'

'I always thought that she was a little too solemn for such a jovial chap as you. You're better off without her, fatty.'

Roland nodded. 'She was solemn. She had this amazingly serious expression, as if she was on the verge of some intense revelation. It took me weeks to work out that she was only wondering which pants to wear.'

Bobby got hold of a stool and pulled it up to the bar to sit on. Roland continued to stand. He seldom sat in pubs, claiming that he was able to drink more standing up. But he was also able to see more, turning to face the prettiest woman as the leaves of an indoor plant will turn to face the light.

'I'm beginning to see what drove you into that register office two years ago. How is the lovely Caroline, by the way?'

'Still lovely.'

'I'd like to get my head wedged so firmly between her legs it would take the sodding fire brigade to get me out.'

'Feel free to discuss my wife. Why don't you get one? Look after them properly, they last for years.'

Roland released a multi-noted belch without a flicker of contrition. He was very proud of his belches: if they had been nominated for an Academy award, you gathered, he wouldn't have been surprised.

'I prefer funerals to weddings,' he said. 'There's something so final about weddings.'

'Not any more.'

'Anyway, the marriage service was written when the life expectancy of the male was thirty-seven. It was never intended to last for years. I'm much too young for it yet. Besides, I'd have to wash every night.'

'There is that.' Bobby looked at the fat friend who called himself his partner and tried to picture him with a bride on his arm.

'Have a whisky,' he said. With closing time approaching, the pub was fuller than ever now, and Bobby moved his stool to make way for some new arrivals.

'Do you know what she is studying?' said one. 'Renaissance literature. She'll be on a bloody course by the time she's forty.'

Roland ignored them. 'Marriage,' he said. 'Milestone or millstone?'

'How should I know,' said Bobby. 'I've only been married for two years.'

'And you're three years younger than me. You were much too young to go. I did warn you.'

'You didn't. You just said that I was flawed by a profound weakness for the opposite sex. I thought that was a bit rich from somebody who bought a Bentley purely to get a better class of customer for his feels-on-wheels service.'

Roland laughed. 'I was getting a bit too old for all that vertical stuff in the town's car parks,' he said.

'You also got rich, of course.'

Bobby derived a malicious enjoyment from references to Roland's wealth. It was the only topic that could discomfort him. He shied away from the subject if it was introduced, and to those people who were curious about the lazy affluence which seemed to surround him, he muttered something about being an entrepreneur. For some reason, it was a very good word for closing a conversation.

The truth was that for fifteen years, starting with a small inheritance from his father, he had involved himself in more than a dozen money-making operations, injecting capital, ideas, and, very occasionally, energy, into wild schemes, all but one of which had repaid him. But his interests enjoyed only short periods of genuine enthusiasm. He began by buying a small café in the country, hiring a chef, and taking it a few places up the social scale. For four weeks he told all telephone inquiries that he was booked up although the place was empty; soon the word got around that The Grotto was the place to dine if only you could get in there. After six months it was heaving every evening, and after a year, Roland, vowing that he would never wash another plate, sold it for three and a half times what he had paid for it.

Soon afterwards he bought 3,000 chickens. Feeding them cost him £1,000 a month, but to everybody's astonishment he still made money. Eventually he decided that there was too much work attached to the upkeep of 3,000 chickens, sold them at a small profit, and started a business called Roland Hodgson Exhibitions Ltd. The money that he made from this venture had almost removed the need for further work. He would hire the biggest hall in a large town and arrange specialist exhibitions: heating, furniture, television and stereo equipment. The exhibitors each paid him handsomely for the

small area of floor space that he allotted them, the public paid at the door for the privilege of coming in, and the sale of the programmes, plus the advertising that they contained, pushed his profit up to not less than £1,000 for a one-day exhibition. On the strength of his trading figures over two years, he sold the firm for £20,000.

The only flop so far in Roland's career as an entrepreneur had been when he thought that he had discovered the new Beatles. He signed up four young men who were known to their remarkably few fans as Chris and the Con Men, renamed them Horror Pudding, spent over £800 on new equipment, new clothes and hiring a recording studio. He had a crazy notion that a wider audience was waiting eagerly for their cacophonous din. But knowing little about pop music, and liking it even less, he found himself in sole charge of a tone-deaf singer, a drummer who was a junkie, and a guitarist who seemed, as the weeks went by, to have arthritis in all eight fingers and at least one thumb. Horror Pudding disbanded amid maximum acrimony, and Roland decided that there was a lot of surplus money going round and round in the twilight world of advertising, some of which should be his. Soon it was. After an ambitious but abortive start as a self-employed copy-writer—'Halitosis is better than no breath at all,' was his most memorable slogan—he bought the rights to the wall advertising in a national chain of steak houses, and sold them immediately for twice as much. Then he turned his attention to newspapers. He travelled round the country buying whole pages in leading provincial newspapers, carved up the space himself and resold it to local advertisers, for whom he wrote wild panegyrics and designed the advert, putting the whole thing out under an eight-column headline which assured anxious readers that the advertisers on this page, if on no other, had been given a coveted seal of approval by some honourable if shadowy group of watchdogs. If a newspaper made £1,000 from its page, Roland made another £1,000 for himself. The travelling involved in this work began eventually to tire him, and he started to look for an investment that would make fewer demands on him or, better still, no demands at all. Within six weeks he had bought a shop, six washing machines, five spin driers and three heavy-duty washers, and opened his first Easy Clean.

Bobby Booth, who had neither the initial advantage of a legacy from his parents—no one in his family had ever left more than a few hundred pounds—nor the bottomless fund of ideas that was evidently housed somewhere in Roland's amorphous bulk, had watched his fat friend's progress with envy from the classroom of a secondary school where he taught English. But just after the first branch of Easy Clean had been successfully opened, two things happened.

The first was professional: the black cloud of depression, which had never been too far away and which a late switch to teaching had shifted only temporarily, was back in full regalia after five years in the classroom. He did not like what teaching appeared to do to a man's personality. Perhaps it came from being irrefutably right for six hours a day; more probably, it stemmed from the daily company of thirty people who quite properly loathed you.

The second thing was personal: he fell in love. The possibility of buying a house—or doing much else—on a teacher's salary did not exist. So he happily accepted Roland's offer when he asked him to manage the launderette for twice his teacher's pay. But he had occasionally regretted it since.

The close ten-year relationship that they had enjoyed was damaged in some way, but whether it was his getting married after helping to knock the product during a thousand drunken evenings together, or whether it was because Roland was now his boss, he wasn't sure. Not that Roland ever referred to himself as Bobby's boss. He called him his partner, as if Bobby had put money into the Easy Clean venture instead of just his life; industrially, Roland was ahead of his time.

'My friend is trying to buy me a drink, Basil,' he said now, holding up his glass. 'All play and no work makes Jack a lively boy.' He handed Basil the glasses and turned to Bobby. 'The idea that work is somehow ennobling is nineteenth-century bosses' propaganda.'

Bobby was feeling warm with the whisky: the world was improving by the minute. 'You've worked pretty hard from time to time,' he said.

'Christ, yes. If I'd got any brains I'd have had a nervous breakdown before now. Cheers.'

'Cheers. Where have you been lately, fatso? What have you been up to apart from not getting your leg over?'

'Looking at property,' said Roland. 'We need some more branches of Easy Clean. You could manage two or three, couldn't you? Of course, it would mean more money.'

'Why don't we go into something interesting? Launderettes are so boring. What about a sex shop? Love aids and all that.'

'Inflatable rubber women, portable splash-proof ceilings. What a great idea! Get yourself a second mortgage and come in on a fifty-fifty basis. Get in on the ground floor!'

'Yeah, and get out in the basement. The people around here are not interested in sex. Apart from you and me. An inflatable rubber woman is just what you need.'

Roland didn't answer. He was surveying the room. Nothing beautiful was going to creep in here without his seeing. Bobby bought two whiskies and two pints of bitter to keep them company.

'How is business?' said Basil, when he had pulled the pints. Basil was fortyish, a tall, lean man with an obsession for stereo equipment. He worked long hours in the Planet, made a lot of money and spent most of it on multiplying oscilloscopes, instrument modules, peak-reading voltmeters, optical tachometers and push-button potentiometers: all this, and a lot more like it, was meat and drink to the four-eyed Basil. Obsessive self-indulgence on this scale offended Bobby in a way he found hard to define, and he struggled to restrict the boundaries of their relationship to ground of his own choosing: he gave Basil money and, conjurer-like, Basil turned it into alcohol.

'Your underwear must be filthy,' Bobby said. 'I never see you in our place.'

'I wash my own,' said Basil. 'Saves money.'

'You wouldn't like it if we started to make our own beer,' said Bobby, but Basil was too busy to pursue the point.

Bobby went to the toilet. Checking the latest graffiti was a peripheral pleasure of trips to Basil's loo. Today's said:

**THE WORLD ENDED YESTERDAY
TODAY IS AN ACTION REPLAY**

Roland had concluded his inventory of the ladies assembled, when he got back.

'You seem a trifle subdued tonight, Robert,' he said, studying Bobby's face. 'Is your lovely lady holding out on you? I know what these wives are like. You don't give bait to fish you've already caught.'

'She's not like that.'

'What's not she like?'

Bobby climbed onto his stool, stared at his two glasses on the counter and chose the whisky. It made him want to discuss it.

'Pull up a chair,' he said.

Uncharacteristically, Roland sat down. 'What's the problem?' he said. 'I can see that you've got one.'

Bobby drank some more whisky. 'I have,' he said. 'I have.'

'Go on.'

'You may or may not be aware that Caroline—that's my wife —is crazy about having kids. Having kids is what marriage is all about to Caroline.'

'I realised that,' Roland said. 'Earth mother.'

'Well, as you may have noticed, given your staggering powers of perception not to mention your fundamentally nosey nature, we have no children.'

'Not any.'

'None.'

'It didn't escape my attention. In fact, I considered giving you a few tips. You have to penetrate the right orifice, you know. All this ramming it in her left ear isn't going to get you anywhere.'

'We only use one.'

'Really? How incredibly boring.'

'We want children.'

'Ah yes.'

Bobby washed the whisky down with some beer and looked at his fat friend.

'We've had some tests,' he said.

'Tests?'

'Yes, tests. To establish the reason for this dearth of tiny feet.'

'And?'

'It's me. I heard today.'

'What—you're impotent?'

'Not impotent, you fool. Sterile.'

Roland put his hand on Bobby's shoulder. 'And you're really fed up about it aren't you?'

'You could say that.'

'I always thought that beneath that granite exterior, there beat a heart of stone.'

'It's Caroline I'm worried about. She wanted children so much. Much more than most wives, I reckon. And she's twenty-seven. She's had a long time to dream about having them. How is she going to react?'

'Doesn't she know yet, then?'

'No. The letter came this morning. She was in the bath when it arrived. I've left it in the kitchen for her to read.'

'I think I'd better buy you a large Bells.'

'Nobody ain't stopping you. She'll probably want a divorce or something.'

'I doubt that it's grounds for divorce. Basil, large Bells. Twice.'

'You don't know my wife. She's a very cool, determined lady.'

They sat in silence with their new drinks.

'Well, you could always adopt,' said Roland eventually. 'I've heard of couples who adopt and promptly have kids of their own.'

Bobby nodded. All day the thought had not occurred to him. He was immediately cheered. 'I expect that's what we will do. Shall we get drunk?'

'I thought we were?'

'Youth is a struggle, manhood a disappointment, old age a disaster. That's what Disraeli meant to say.'

'Bilgewater,' Roland said. 'Life is there to be fought, old fruit. Don't give me any of that doomy, neurotic hogswash. Piss on the doomvendors. You have to get off your arse and get stuck in.'

'How can we lose when we're so sincere?' Bobby said.

Walking home through the rain at midnight, he composed his features into the correct shape for a late arrival. It was only a

17

five-minute walk, and he ignored the rain and counted the Christmas trees in the front windows; the country might be going bankrupt but around here there was a public determination to enjoy the festivities.

The estate to which he had taken his bride two years before had sprung up almost overnight on the edge of the town like so many mushrooms. A red-faced old farmer, who had spent the best years of his life dispensing potatoes to most of the county, had suddenly found himself a quarter of a millionaire after two trips to the local council's planning department. Today three vast potato fields had become the Heatherside Estate: dozens of sandy-coloured boxes, some with green roofs, some with red, some with yellow garage doors and some with blue, but all of them built to the same design and none of them having more than the acceptable minimum in the way of garden space. Bobby, launderette manager, had paid £8,000 for the house with a twenty-five year mortgage. As a teacher he would still be renting a flat. The house was now worth £14, 500, and to his surprise Caroline loved it. She loved its newness, its modern kitchen, the way it was laid out. New houses did not have picture rails and other dust traps; women voted for them.

The lights were still on downstairs which might or might not be a good sign. If Caroline was working she would be happy; but today there were other reasons why she could be waiting up for him.

He unlocked the front door and called: 'Hallo! Nice to see me.'

She called, 'Hallo,' and he went into the front room where she was sitting at the big table with her typewriter. She was wearing a green blouse which went well with her long blonde hair and tight white jeans. He went across and kissed her on the forehead; she looked stunning.

'Keep at it, kid,' he said. 'You'll soon be able to keep me in the manner to which I hope to become accustomed.'

She had worked on a women's magazine before their marriage, and was now retained on a freelance basis to write the advice column, 'Ask Susan Smith'. Every week at least fifty questions from troubled readers would arrive from the magazine's London office, and Caroline would compile her page

18

from a dozen of them. Her advice, what Bobby saw of it, seemed to belong to the 'masturbation makes you blind' school of thought, and he often wondered why people continued to consult the oracle when the best they could hope for was a rap over the knuckles for behaviour, or merely thoughts, which infringed no rules that Bobby knew of. (After a few drinks he had once cheered himself up by firing off a bizarre query to Susan Smith. It had begun: 'I am a forty-nine-year-old virgin with a wooden leg.' But it was evidently not a predicament which Susan Smith felt capable of alleviating.)

'I've nearly finished,' she said now. Her soft voice had a slight West-Country accent. 'Have you been drinking with Roland?' Like most wives, she was apt to blame her husband's friends for his waywardness.

'Well, we did have one or two in the Planet. Then Basil wouldn't let us out at closing time. He locked the doors and kept forcing alcohol down our throats.'

'You're stewed?'

'Nonsense. Get on with your work.'

He picked up her copy of *The Times* and determined to stay quiet. For five or six hours work as Susan Smith, Caroline received £50 a week.

He read the headlines: Cultural Dilemmas of French Communism. Not quite the late-night reading he required. Blow Jobs For 200. *Blow Jobs For 200?* No, Jobs Blow For 200. He had drunk more whisky than he thought.

'I see Laos has devalued the kip,' he said. There was no reply. A confused but hopelessly pregnant schoolgirl in Wigan was obviously about to get the you-should-have-thought-of-that-before treatment. He returned to the newspaper. Horsehair for violin bows was getting scarce—it was one thing after another.

'Good Lord!' he said. 'A foot square block of ice has fallen into a garden in Dorset.'

'Really?'

'Apparently it's frozen urine. I wonder who's been having a pee up there?'

He looked up but he had lost his audience.

'The lab report says that God's got diabetes.'

Caroline turned to him from the typewriter. 'Why don't

you go into the other room and watch television? I won't be long. I want us to have a long talk tonight.'

'A talk?'

'About you-know-what.'

'Oh.'

He didn't feel quite so merry now, but the whisky helped. He turned obediently to the television page to see what delights were beaming their way through the rain to be captured by the Reg Butler creation on his roof: it was a two-act opera based on a Kafka novel, roughly equivalent in enjoyment-potential, he imagined, to standing on your head for a couple of hours in a barrel of cow dung. He put the paper down.

The room in which they were sitting looked rather like a furniture shop window. Only the people in it were more than a couple of years old. The green wall-to-wall carpet and the new, modern furniture looked barely used. The grey-patterned wallpaper was immaculate; even the 'antique' clock on the marble mantelpiece was new, a tiny battery at the back being its source of power. The whole effect, he had found to his surprise, was deeply offensive to certain friends who were burdened with an elusive attribute called taste. But to Bobby, after the rougher surroundings of his bachelor days—one-bar electric fires that just about kept the toadstools off the ceiling— it was all luxury, his first proper home even if home was where the final demands are.

He stood up and went over to his wife.

'You're a very sensuous lady,' he said. It wasn't just her sleepy eyes, her full lips, her magnificent breasts, her trim bottom; even her full nose was somehow erotic. He wondered whether he could postpone the talk by making love.

'I fancy you something horrible.'

'He said with that refinement of thought and elegance of diction which never seemed to desert him,' she quoted.

'My goodness, Caroline, it's a business doing pleasure with you.'

He was reluctant to leave her: a new mood would have to be created later if he went upstairs now.

'Do you think your magazine would like to serialise my life story?' he asked. 'We could get it ghosted by some hack. As told to T. S. Eliot. I've got a few titles ready. How about

Hard Up With A Hard-on?'

'Go to bed, darling. I won't be long.'

He put his hands on her shoulders and leaned over to see what she had written: 'It may interest J.L. of Hampshire to know that twenty per cent of all women—one in five—never attain orgasm. Its frequency is related to social class, upbringing, education, previous attitudes. The better the education and the higher the social class, the greater the frequency of orgasm.'

He kissed the top of her head and marvelled at the information it contained.

'I'll see you later,' he said, and the black cloud of depression had returned.

He had woken up one morning and decided to find a wife. The decision, sudden and urgent, had followed a disturbed night during which he had woken several times with feverish images dancing spastically across his mind: a plane in a storm, a black man in a wheelchair, his father's grave. It was four days after his thirtieth birthday.

The previous day he had read an article about bachelors in one of the popular newspapers; it had set out to bury the carefree, happy-go-lucky image of the single man. Avoiding the marriage trap used to be an achievement for a man, it said. Not any more. The recent, presumably regrettable, shortage of world wars meant that the men were no longer outnumbered by lovely and eager young women. In fact, there were 60,000 more men than women in the twenty to twenty-four age group. That and equal pay had transformed the young ladies of Britain from desperate husband-hunters into selective independent creatures. Then there was the Pill.

'The Samaritans organisation, which gets phone calls from people with desperate problems, reports that 28 per cent of their calls from men are from single men,' said the article. 'Yet only 17.5 per cent of the male adult population is single. A National Council of Social Service spokesman said: "Until now it has largely been women who have led lonely lives of desperation and despair. But in the future, lonely unmarried men will be a major problem." '

He was about to become a major problem. The first danger-sign had been when he suddenly discovered that he was slow-ing down, if not actually stopping, outside the windows of women's clothes shops, to enjoy the briefness of the new bathing costumes, or the cleavage revealed by the new cut-away blouses. It could only be a short step from here, he decided, to becoming the latest in a long line of phantom pantie snatchers, scourge of the district's washing lines, the man in the Maidenform bra.

He was no longer in his twenties, and each year was shorter than the last. What did the future hold for him—apart from a few late-night calls to the Samaritans? Retracing his footsteps, it was hard to see where he had gone wrong.

He had enjoyed many affairs with women, some of them torrid, most of them tepid, but after months or weeks he had always found himself wondering: Is this all there is to it? He used to look at the way that the human race had so com-placently paired off to see if any couple could show him what he was missing; but he could not avoid the feeling that most people had settled for a lot less than the grand passion that he had been vainly seeking.

He developed a cynical attitude to the subject and changed girlfriends more often. He became known as a bachelor rather than a potential husband. 'A woman's place is in the wrong,' he would say. 'Women should look like women and act like men.' Their behaviour was the kernel of his problem because he could not comprehend their blind anxiety to wed. It seemed to him that few men ever made a decision quite so far-reaching as a woman's choice of husband. It settled her standard of living for good—the quality of the food she would eat, the clothes she would wear, the holidays she would have. It decided whether she would live in luxury or penury, in a mansion or a back street. And yet they rushed into it with far less caution than a man would show in a penny card game. Girls just wanted a husband, any husband, he decided. They lacked the discrimination of a flea looking for a dog.

He remembered driving out into the country with a happy, dark-haired secretary with whom he had enjoyed a passionate affair for all of ten days. She had nearly tipped him over the brink, but all he could remember about her now was that she had pubic hairs like a Brillo pad.

'Are you going to marry me?' she had asked ominously, when they had left the town behind. 'If not, there's no point in continuing with this.'

Frivolity, as usual, was his armour.

'You couldn't give me up, just like that, could you?'

'Try me.'

'And yet you'd marry me?'

'Yes please.'

He looked at her and realised that she meant it.

'I don't understand women.'

'No, you don't.'

He never went out with her again and she became gloomily attached to a succession of bearded young men who between them wiped the smile off her face for ever.

By the time he was twenty-eight, women had begun to appear less in his life. He was putting a lot of work into his new career as a teacher, and he joked that when he had been out of work and had time for women, he didn't have the money, and now that he had the money, he did not have the time. He noticed them often enough, caught their perfume in a crowd, but sexual intercourse, which he had once taken for granted, began to assume the wild magic of an unreachable luxury. At a time when he had expected that lovely ladies would increasingly succumb, willingly or not, to his mature charm, they became strangely elusive, on occasions impossible to find, as if the word had got around that he would waste their time, use their bodies, break their hearts. And the best were already sold: show me a pretty face, he used to think, and I'll show you a wedding ring. The alarming truth dawned gradually: any girl of twenty-five or over had been sexually rejected by a generation and left—gladly—for him, the late man at the sale. (Not that in the first flush of youthful enthusiasm that followed the discovery that girls wanted to do it too, he had been a bull at a gate, despite his Taurus star sign. A kindly aunt had told him as a boy: 'Never run after a woman or a bus—there will always be another one along.' The advice had reached him at a receptive and undiscerning age and, taking it literally, he had subsequently spent, it seemed to him, a disproportionate amount of his formative years waiting at bus stops, usually in the rain, with an erection like a lead weight in his pants.)

Like most frustrated men, he began to get a distorted picture of the opposite sex. He became a masto-concupiscent, convinced in the lonely hours of the night that if a woman had a really monumental pair of breasts, he would happily forgive her anything: hairy armpits, halitosis, flatulence, clap. He staggered through wild, whisky-flavoured dreams about ladies with cavernous bosoms, the sort of chest equipment that made it necessary to shout. 'What do you want to drink—drink—drink?' The words echoed around the mammary mountain that stood between them. When the obsession reached its peak, he began to resent that women covered themselves up; their very clothes were a rejection directed at him. He decided that for a woman to own a really large pair of breasts and not to show them, from time to time, to anybody who fancied a guided tour, was like someone possessing a Goya and hoarding it in the privacy of their home without loaning it out occasionally to a public gallery.

Would the erotic highlight of his life centre soon on the tatty raincoat and the bi-weekly flash on the Bakerloo line? Getting and egg into a decanter was beginning to seem marginally easier than the insertion which blocked his mind. Encouraged by the literary efforts of his English class, he toyed with the idea of compiling what would undoubtedly become the definitive work on sexual frustration. He made a list of possible titles: *The Art of Masturbation* wasn't racy enough. *Rub-A-Dub-Dub* was a bit pop. He settled for *The Blurred Hand*.

The problem grew. It was discussed nightly in the Planet.

'Perhaps I need a wife,' said Bobby eventually.

Roland was appalled. 'Look, if only one person in sixty is a pretty girl it still means that there are one million of them on this island somewhere,' he said.

'Which bugger's hiding them?' asked Bobby.

'Yes, well, this joint isn't exactly a granary of crumpet, I agree. Perhaps you're mixing in the wrong circles, old fruit.'

Bobby looked around the room. There were one or two pretty girls among the crowd, but all of them attached.

'What about the new barmaid?' he asked.

A small black-haired girl had been hired that week by Basil, and like her many predecessors was being eagerly propositioned by a group of drinkers.

Roland was disdainful. 'She looks a bit grubby to me,' he said. 'Her today, gonorrhoea tomorrow.'

'Well, I wouldn't climb over her to get to you.'

'In this mood, Robert, you'd regard a buffalo's left ear as an erogenous zone.'

Bobby drank his whisky. Frustrated was when every girl seemed pretty. It was easy for Roland. With spare time and spare money, he was getting his share, all right; the trouble was that he was getting Bobby's share, as well.

'Now you're over thirty, fatty, do you ever get to wondering what the girl you'll eventually marry is up to tonight?' he asked. 'It's a pretty disquieting thought—your wife out there somewhere up to God knows what tricks with some pox doctor's clerk.'

'Listen fartface, the word marriage is not in my dictionary. It's very worrying the way you mention it more and more. You need straightening out. Get your leg over by all means, but we don't want any of this poncing up the aisle. You know what Noël Coward called marriage? The aftermath of love.'

Rotund Roland looked pleased with his demolition job, but Bobby was no longer convinced; the doubts were losing to the desires. He examined the doubts. He could see the advantages of being hooked on a woman, he could see the delights; but how time-consuming it would be, admiring her beauty! She would be gorgeous to look at, of course, but how much would he have to kick out of his life to accommodate her? And would fixing shelves beat playing snooker? Would discussing the boring neighbours beat drinking pints? Would watching her lovely body drift around the room be eventually more beneficial to discussing money-raising schemes in the Planet with whoever had one? He could see short-term benefits, but what about the long term?

But a few weeks later, as his thirtieth birthday slipped past on a costly river of Guinness and whisky, the doubts were washed away with it.

His first move to find a wife—to unearth just one of the one million pretty ladies who were evidently around somewhere—involved no more effort than a letter to a marriage bureau. The reply was brisk.

25

'We charge a registration fee of £17.50 plus £1.75 VAT,' it said. 'When you marry, a fee of £35 plus £3.50 VAT is payable if you marry a client of ours.'

The idea of paying Value Added Tax on a bride seemed to take the ring-a-ding out of it somehow.

His second move was to mix in different circles. He cut his nightly visits to the Planet down to two a week. Roland was suspicious. Bobby told him that he had examination papers to check.

He went to the International Club where au pairs with strange accents gathered once a week to sip fruit juice and listen to records. It was unlikely that they were looking for English husbands but he met a few of them, two Danish girls, a French girl and a strapping young lady from Munich. On his third visit, the summer dress began to emerge and he was reminded unwillingly of the Continental fascination for unshaven armpits; he did not go again. He transferred his loyalty briefly to a new discotheque in the town centre, but in the flashing lights which were in vogue at the time it was difficult to tell the girls from the boys and the volume of the music made it impossible to ask. He tried other public houses to see if there were any with what he would regard as a satisfactory male/female ratio among the customers; there were not. And then, just when he was deciding that much more drastic action was going to be necessary, his wife walked in.

He was taking a break from the conventional English lesson, and trying to discover how much general knowledge the thirty-two long-haired louts who made up his very own form were carrying around with them. Name the American presidents since the war. Which is the second largest country in the world? Is Edinburgh west of Liverpool? Which party has won the most elections since 1945? Stuff like this, he found, invariably hooked an age group that had been reared on television quiz shows, and he had their total attention for a change when the headmaster walked in.

He was not at all the archetypal headmaster, or, at any rate, the sort of headmaster who had plagued Bobby's school career: small, wizened, pedantic, vicious. He was a big, ugly man, not much more than forty, who had once been a minor star in the rugby firmament.

'Ah, Mr Booth,' he said. 'I've got a girl coming along this afternoon from a women's magazine. She is writing an article on something or other, and I've agreed to give her the run of a class for an hour or so. I thought yours. They're about the age she wants.'

'Okay,' said Bobby. 'What time?'

'She's coming at three. I'll bring her to you then.' At five past three the headmaster returned with Caroline. Bobby stopped looking for a wife.

Only two of the three bedrooms upstairs were furnished. The third room was the smallest, and they had expected nine months' notice from the first occupant, although Caroline had called it the nursery from the day they moved in. The second bedroom had a carpet and a double bed that had arrived from Bobby's bachelor flat. Both were rejected by Caroline who wanted a new double bed and a new carpet. It was never discussed but he understood her unspoken suspicions that both carpet and bed had witnessed constant scenes of unbridled debauchery that were over for good and going to remain unmentioned in his pre-Caroline past; he was too flattered to disabuse her. The room contained nothing else. Furnishing it was at the bottom of their list of priorities.

Their own bedroom at the front of the house was the biggest. The centre of it was their large and luxurious double bed to which they had come originally as lovers, but, more recently, as increasingly desperate athletes, varying tactics, times and techniques to achieve the elusive goal of impregnation. Susan Smith's cheques had paid for the handsome dressing-table which stretched along most of one wall, and Bobby had built the wardrobe which completely covered another. On his side of the bed there was a lamp and a transistor radio; on her side, a lamp and a Teasmade. Last year's Christmas present, he remembered now, which raised another problem: what was he going to buy her this year?

He took all his clothes off, hung up his jeans in the wardrobe, threw his sweater on the bed, and dropped everything else into the huge Ali Baba linen basket that stood in one corner. In the full-length mirror his body looked like the same tall, lithe body that had scored a thousand runs, hit a

27

hundred goals and turned on twenty-two grateful ladies in the last decade and a half. But it wasn't. It was older, it was slower and now, the news had arrived, it was flawed. This body was not going to reproduce itself.

He took a towel and went into the bathroom for a shower. There had been a time when he could go happily to bed with feet that were a long way short of fresh; nowadays the nightly foot-wash was the penalty of nuptial bliss. There were one or two other bits that he had to watch as well. He went to bed clean these days all right. The trouble was that all this late water freshened him up so that sometimes he lay awake for hours, as clean as a surgeon's knife.

When he returned to the bedroom, Caroline was undressing. He wondered whether she had hoped to slip into bed before he had finished his shower. Even now she was embarrassed by her nudity and also by his. He had been puzzled by it at first, and it had taken him weeks to persuade her to sleep naked; but afterwards, when the Susan Smith fan letters began to arrive, he discovered that plenty of husbands had never even seen their wives in the nude.

He sat on the bed and watched her slip out of her jeans. His penis lept dutifully to attention.

'You've got lovely legs,' he said. She was trying to keep the temperature down by keeping the wardrobe door between them but it swung open and she gave it up. When she was naked she had to turn round. Her breasts hardly sagged at all and he loved them and the rest of her: the short fleshy legs that he had once devoted an hour to kissing, the bottom that was the silkiest he had touched, the jet-black thatch of pubic hair that contrasted so stunningly with the blonde hair on her head.

'What's *that* doing pointing at the ceiling?' she asked.

'I can't understand it,' he said. 'Come here.'

But she walked past him and slipped into bed, pulling the covers quickly to her chin. He climbed over her and got into bed himself, propping himself up on an elbow to look down at her thoughtful face.

He wanted to confuse the issue by making love, but he could see that she did not want it. When she wanted it, she smiled. Her sexual past had remained a mystery to him and he was happy to leave it like that. Incredibly, they had not made love until after their wedding, but they had got married so quickly that he had hardly noticed: celibacy, by that time, was a way of life. She was not a virgin—there were no virgins —but West-Country girls were in his experience as sexually backward as Irish girls and he would not have been surprised if she had lost her virginity riding a horse. He didn't care to ask. Her sexual past had remained a mystery because he was scared of not liking what he heard. She was strangely shy, though, and he found her shyness exciting even though sometimes he wasn't sure whether she was satisfied. Lately, wanting children, she had encouraged him a lot and the shyness was beginning to fall away. Once, to his astonishment, they had done it standing up in the kitchen, but his secret delight that his quiet, beautiful girl had suddenly been transformed into a sex bomb did not last. She had heard, or been told, or read somewhere that vertical intercourse increased the chances of pregnancy.

So long as his lust matched her vision of nappies and prams the bedroom was a lovely place to be. But today it was different.

He put his hand under the covers to find her body. She was lying on her back, with her eyes closed.

'We made love last night,' she said.

'As long ago as that?' The remark and the tone annoyed him.

'I want to talk.' She opened her eyes and looked up at him.

'I want to kiss your bum.'

She closed her eyes again. 'We seem to have a conflict of interests here,' she said.

'Dear Susan Smith, I want to hold serious conversations with my husband, but all he wants to do is kiss my bum.'

'Why are you avoiding the subject, Bobby?'

'I've got an erection up to my nose. I can't concentrate. I'm very concerned about the frequency of orgasm among launderette managers. What subject?'

'Go into the bathroom and masturbate, dear. It will be good for your automatic watch.'

The remark—so uncharacteristic—shocked him mildly. 'Good Lord, is that the sort of advice Susan Smith is handing out? The watch is on the wrong wrist, anyway. What subject?'

'The subject of us. Children. What we are going to do.'

'Oh that.' He lay back on the bed, defeated. Sometimes it was Caroline who sounded like the ex-teacher. She could introduce a firm note into her voice that he had never managed. 'Well, you want to talk about it, beautiful. What do you want to say?'

But his eyes were closed as he thought regretfully about his one big mistake: agreeing to the fertility tests. He had never liked submitting himself to any medical examination; you never knew what unpleasant truths the men in the white coats might impart. And the fertility test idea had seemed absurdly premature. They had been married for less than two years then. It was a little early to worry over-much about the empty nursery. The whole subject of sterility anyway was riddled with a certain brutal humour that he found off-putting: *'I'm afraid you have albumen in your water, Mr Brown, and your wife has sugar in hers. Why don't you forget about having a family and open a candy floss store?'*

Caroline suggested the tests one sunny autumn morning and then pursued the idea with a relentlessness that surprised him. For two months he prevaricated, but it was a losing battle against her implacable will. He gave in eventually for the reason, he was discovering, that men do give in when a determined wife keeps the pressure up—for peace. And now he wished that he had not.

She made an appointment with their own doctor at the health clinic, and they visited him together one evening. He was a white-haired old gentleman called Grimshaw who, after a lifetime in the business, brought the same expressionless mien to everything from cancer to corns. The range of his questions surprised them: childhood ailments, accidents, operations, psychological problems, length of courtship, their honeymoon, what type of contraception they had ever used and for how long, length and frequency of intercourse and, to Bobby, had he ever wet the bed?

Then he examined them individually. Caroline waited outside, while Doctor Grimshaw brought his inquisitive fingers to work on Bobby.

'Have you any reason to believe that you may have caused any conceptions at any time?' he asked, during a painful but fruitless search for hernias. Bobby said that he had not, but the doctor looked sceptical.

'Get dressed,' he said, and went over to a wall cupboard from which he produced a small, lidded jar. 'I can't find anything wrong with you physically,' he said, 'so what we will need is a sample of your semen.'

'What now?' said Bobby. 'I don't think—'

'Whenever you like,' said Doctor Grimshaw briskly. 'Just take it to the pathology laboratory at the hospital within two hours of production. They'll have your papers. Send Mrs Booth in, please.'

It was almost an hour before they finally left.

'That was awful,' said Caroline, flushed.

'What did he do?'

'What *didn't* he do! My God! He went over me inch by inch.'

'Lucky man.'

She was laughing about it now.

'He palpated my pelvic fossa, if you want to know. Looking for ovarian anomalies.'

'How rude.'

They started to walk home.

'What on earth is that?' said Caroline.

'That there is a sterile jar. I am going to make love to it. It may replace you in my life if it's any good.'

'Well, it doesn't look very attractive to me.'

'Nor me. Are you sure you want to go through with this?'

He was hoping that she was regretting what she had started, that she had had enough.

'Of course,' she said.

Protracted bouts of private hilarity accompanied the next problem: how to get the sperm into the jar. It seemed to Bobby, when he came to consider it, that he would require, at the very least, the practised skills of a masturbating darts champion, or a much larger jar, or some wifely assistance. After a few days, he got to wondering how this delicate matter was dealt with elsewhere, notably down on the farm. They were hoarding bulls' semen as if bulls were on the way out, but how did they get it in the first place? The earnest laboratory technician who set off across a windy field to offer a hand job to an angry bull would surely be discovered soon afterwards upside down in a hedge clutching a broken test tube.

Then Roland told him about the facsimile cow.

'It's made of steel,' he said. 'They cover it with cow hide to fool the bull. The bull mounts the facsimile cow, gives it one, and inside is a brave little man who collects the juice.'

'Sounds more like a fucksimile cow to me,' Bobby had said.

Caroline began to get edgy. The sterile jar remained empty. Her victory was slipping away.

'When are you going to do it?' she asked.

'You've got to get into the mood for that sort of thing,' Bobby said. 'It's not a very attractive jar, after all. Couldn't you stick a nude picture on the side, just to get me going?'

But when he woke up the following morning in his customary tumescent condition, Caroline and jar were ready.

'If you won't do it, I will,' she said.

He lay on his back, half asleep, and smiled up at her.

'You do it awfully well,' he said.

She pulled the covers back to lay the jar on his stomach. It was cold. He closed his eyes.

'Don't you go to sleep,' said Caroline. 'Concentrate. This is business, not pleasure. Are you nearly there?'

'I'm going to make it last.'

'You are not,' she said, and began to rub faster. But when he came suddenly she was caught unawares and the sperm splattered over the Teasmade a yard away.

'Christ,' said Caroline. 'I didn't know it shot out like that.'

Bobby lay still. 'What a sheltered life you've led. How much do I owe you?'

He was laughing, but she was not. When he left for work she was sulking. But by the time he got home her attitude had changed. She had found out how it was done from a neighbour whose husband had had a vasectomy.

Her welcome was seductive. She was wearing a short skirt that Bobby loved and she hated, and no stockings.

'What's all this?' he asked, running his hand up the back of her leg.

'Come and sit down, darling. I've got a nice big steak for you and a bottle of wine.'

'Is it my birthday?'

'I've cracked it,' she said. 'The mystery of how to fill the jar.'

'How do you?'

'You use one of these.' She held up a packet of Durex contraceptives. 'You just empty it into the jar afterwards.'

'Why didn't we think of that?'

Two weeks later, Caroline was given an appointment at the gynaecological clinic, but before she could keep it, a letter arrived from Doctor Grimshaw. It said that the results of Bobby's sperm test were abnormal, and more would be needed. An appointment to see a genito-urinary specialist would follow.

When Bobby attended the hospital, he was submitted to the same examination that he had endured at the hands of Doctor Grimshaw. At the end of it, he was told that he would have to be admitted to hospital overnight for further tests. A week later, equipped with his first pair of pyjamas for fourteen years, he reported yet again to the hospital and was shown to a small ward which he shared with two empty beds and a surly young man who declined to reveal the reason for his visit. A testicular biopsy was performed in the evening.

When he went home the following day, he was still no wiser about why he had no children. But a week later the letter arrived from Doctor Grimshaw, who had received the surgeon's report.

Spermatazoa were absent from the seminiferous tubules, it said. This indicated total sterility.

That was the little time-bomb that had arrived in the post that morning.

When Caroline finally spoke it was as if she had spent days, if not weeks, thinking out exactly what she was going to say.

'You've often told me what a prim and proper young lady I am when you are modern and permissive, so what I am going to say shouldn't shock you at all, except that it's me saying it.'

Bobby lay back at attention, eyes still closed, hands on thighs. 'And what are you going to say, fishface?'

'I must have a baby.'

'I know, Caroline. I know you want a baby. And you shall have a baby. But it's a bit too soon for us to have looked into the subject yet, isn't it? We only got Grimshaw's letter this morning. I'm still reeling from that. But we'll get on to it. There are several ways of adopting children.'

There was an ominous silence. Bobby filled it. 'The funny thing is that couples who can't have children and adopt one, often have their own children afterwards.'

Caroline's voice sounded a long way away. 'That is only when it was the woman at fault,' she said.

He realised that she was right, and that he was trespassing on Susan Smith territory.

'Well, you must know all about adoption,' he said finally. 'Who handles it, and so on.'

There was another silence broken only by the rain on the windows.

'Bobby, I don't want to adopt someone else's baby.'

The statement, delivered quietly, almost apologetically, was a whiplash across his consciousness. He had a feeling of ground shifting, of positions being lost.

'What are you implying?' he asked eventually.

'What are you inferring?'

'I'm not inferring anything yet. I'm not following your drift.'

'You're not?'

'You've got the most ambiguous drift I've ever come across.'

Suddenly she sat up in bed. 'I want my own baby,' she said. '*My* baby out of *my* body.'

She started to cry.

Bobby, as surprised by her tears as by what she had said, lay inertly below her.

'I'm perfectly capable of having my own children,' she said from behind a handkerchief. 'Oh, it's not fair.'

She slumped down on the bed again, burying her face in the pillow like a child, her golden hair mingling with the tears and her body racked by sobs.

TWO

He dreamed a joke: a letter to *The Times* claimed to have spotted the first cuckold of the year. He also dreamed a solution: artificial insemination. It was a nightmare of a dream in which Caroline had filled the house with prams and cots, and was knitting baby clothes so quickly that he stumbled round thigh-deep in wool. He took her back to Doctor Grimshaw, who had an Afro hairstyle and a long black beard, to discuss artificial insemination. But there was a disastrous mix-up on the crowded shelves of the hospital's laboratory. Caroline gave birth to a chimpanzee.

When he woke up it was Christmas Eve. A weak sun had replaced the rain. Caroline slept. He slipped out of bed as usual to open the launderette before breakfast. Only the newsagents were open before him. He went into one of them to buy some cigarettes and a paper. The headlines were familiar: Premier Hits Out. He unlocked the launderette and found one letter on the mat. He went on in, put on the lights, put change, five pences and ten pences, in the change machine, and lit a cigarette. He could remember when he would never smoke before breakfast.

The streets outside were still wet, but empty. Usually there was a good early-morning trade from people who had to do their washing before work but perhaps today, being Christmas Eve, would be different. He picked up the paper to see who the Premier was Hitting Out at, and then he remembered the letter. He did not recognise the handwriting on the envelope, but that was not unusual; letters to his establishment were written by the owners of one red sock, or the former owners of a pair of gold cuff-links or even, on one occasion, a wedding ring. This communication, however, did not fall into that category. It was a Christmas card sent, according to the ornate print-work on the front, to The Man I Love. He opened it quickly. In the same handwriting as on the envelope was the

35

unsigned question: How can we lose when we're so sincere?

He tore it up almost nervously and dropped it into the wastepaper basket beneath his desk. Caroline looked in often enough when she was shopping—it was not the sort of mail that she was going to enthuse about. He tried to remember the girl who had come in the previous evening but he could not even summon up a picture of her face. Only the full T-shirt had been retained in his memory bank. But the irony of an attractive girl sending him a coy come-on now that he was married depressed him. Where had she been, he wondered, during that long priapic period of his life when girls had been harder to find than a gang-bang in the Vatican? Today she was a complication that he no longer needed, and the card was already forgotten when he left the shop.

He walked home to breakfast trying to absorb a little of the Christmas atmosphere which was presumably around. It was a bit early for the carol-singers, but the Chamber of Commerce lights were already on, a twinkling reminder to the public to spend, and there was a bunch of mistletoe hanging expectantly over the door of the Evelyn Beauty Clinic (Youthifying Eye Treatments for fluid retention and muscular slackness—£2).

Caroline was cooking breakfast when he got back. Breakfast used to be a coffee, but since taking over the launderette the early-morning walk into town had given him a fresh appetite. They took it in the kitchen on a tiny white table. For some reason it was the only meal they ate there.

He sat down to a plateful of bacon, tomatoes, mushrooms and two eggs, and wondered whether to return to the subject of last night.

'What am I going to buy you for Christmas?' he asked.

Caroline, in blue jeans this morning with a tartan shirt, put some toast down in front of him and sat down to drink her coffee. She shrugged. She was still thinking of last night.

'How about a car?' he said. He was beginning to think that perhaps outrageous generosity could compensate for his deficiency.

'I can't drive, darling.'

'You could learn.'

'What do we need a car for? We only live 200 yards from

36

town. Buy me a crate of Beefeater Gin. I think I'll take up drinking like you.'

He looked across the table and saw a sadness in her eyes that frightened him.

'Cheer up, C,' he said. 'Hey, we're going to a party tonight.'

'Whose party?'

Caroline had never been enthusiastic about the alcoholic orgy conducted on licensed premises, but when the same thing was transferred to a private house and called a party she had been known to lead the singing.

'Roland's. It's at his place. Everybody's going.'

'That'll be nice.' She smiled for the first time. 'I'm sorry I was in such a mood last night.'

'I dreamed about it.'

'What did you dream?'

'I dreamed the solution to our problem. AID.'

'Artificial insemination? No, thank you.'

'Why not? You said you want your own baby. You meant what you said last night?'

'I meant it.'

'Well, there's the answer,' said Bobby. He regretted that the subject had been brought up, but now that it had he was determined to be businesslike.

Caroline drank her coffee and stared at, or through, the table. 'It might have big ears or red hair or something.'

'What might?'

'My baby. I'd want to know who the father was. I'd want to *pick* the father, like every other girl.' She took her cup over to the sink and turned on the hot tap. 'I suppose that sounds unreasonable to you?'

'Not at all. I'll put an advert in the paper. What are we looking for? What type of daddy are we after? Big, blond, Nordic? Short, dark, swarthy? Athlete? Aesthete? Brains? Brawn? Give me a clue and I'll see what we can produce.'

'*We* can't produce anything. That's the trouble.'

He got up and walked over to the sink. The question required some courage.

'Caroline, do you want a divorce?'

She turned to face him and then took his hand. Her answer made his eyes burn. 'I'd have to be crazy to divorce a lovely man like you.'

'Well, I don't feel very lovely at the moment.'

'You look awfully lovely to me. Go to work.'

'No divorce?'

'Of course not. I don't want a divorce. I want a baby.'

Bobby nodded very slowly.

'I think I'm getting your message,' he said.

Walking back to the shop, he imagined Caroline snatching a baby from a pram; there was a lot of it going on. He could see himself arriving home one evening to find her nursing a baby by the fire, and pleading with him to keep her secret from the world.

At the launderette, somebody had hung an out-of-order notice on one of the washing machines, and a woman who seemed to wash the underwear of the entire British army was complaining that there were no plastic bags in the plastic-bag machine. Bobby dealt with her, spent half an hour fixing the machine, and then phoned Roland. Della, his secretary, answered.

'He hasn't arrived yet, Bobby,' she said.

'What time are you expecting him?'

'I don't know. He hasn't come in yesterday yet.'

'Very amusing. Tell him I rang.'

Two washing machines juddered to a stop, but there was nobody in to empty them. He took the clothes out and put them in one of the yellow plastic buckets that were used to carry clean but wet clothes to the driers. He did all this in the usual work trance. It sometimes seemed hard to believe that he had been put on this spinning globe—the latest, most refined product of a million years of evolution—to watch people clean their underwear; the fact that most of his fellow tenants were engaged in equally fatuous pursuits for the whole of their active lives did nothing to allay the niggling worm in his brain. But society, in his neck of the woods, anyway, attached greater value to clean clothes than to the education of a hundred children and he would learn to adjust in the end. What always surprised him was that his regrets about the current values seemed to be shared by nobody.

The telephone rang in his office.

'Morning, fartface,' Roland said. 'What's the matter? Have we been robbed?'

'Robbed? No. I thirst.'

'Blimey, they don't open for another half-hour.'

'Last one at the bar's a cissy.'

'Okay, I'll see you there. This is going to be a *very* heavy day. Caroline coming to the party?'

'Of course. Who else is?'

'Everybody. See you in the Planet at half past.'

An earnest young man was waiting for him outside, clutching a postcard which he wanted to pin on the launderette's notice board. The board was beginning to replace the local newspaper as a source of information about what was going on. The postcard was an invitation to audition for the operatic society's production of 'The Pirates of Penzance'. Already on the board were invitations to the film society, the art society, the chess club, which Bobby belonged to, the Young Conservatives, the archaeological society, the amateur dramatic society, the ramblers' club, the cycling club, the Baptist church and something mysteriously called the do-it-yourself circle. But in the interests of customer relations, Bobby still found room for the message to the town's would-be opera stars.

Walking across the square to the Planet took at least three times longer than usual. The shops were about to close for two days so the British shopper was out in a panic, laying in supplies that would survive a seven-week siege.

Roland was sitting alone at the bar, completing the *Telegraph* crossword.

'I thought you were going to beat me here?' he said.

'It's the crowds,' said Bobby. 'There's nine million people out there, fighting for bread. Morning, Basil.'

Basil pulled him a pint of lager which seemed a harmless enough start to the drinking that was to come. Roland was drinking bitter.

'So why the early boozing?' he asked. 'Some problem.'

'You could say that. You could put it that way.'

'Caroline.'

'She wants a baby.'

'Well, I knew that.'

'No, listen. She wants a baby. Give birth to it. She was actually crying last night for the first time since we got married.'

'She doesn't want to adopt?'

'Refuses.'

'Well, there's always artificial insemination.'

'I thought of that. She won't have it. She says she wants to pick the father.'

'Do you mean that she is looking for a man to give her one? If so, my credentials are of the highest.'

'Well, it might be a laugh to you, fatso, but that's not how it looks to me.'

'Is she serious?'

'We've sort of talked round the subject, but I'm pretty certain that that is what's at the back of her mind.'

'She wants to find a man who'll make her pregnant?'

'It's beginning to sound that way.'

Roland whistled. 'I can hardly believe it,' he said. 'Not Caroline.'

'Oh, it's got nothing to do with sex. She wants to breed.'

'Even so.'

Roland extracted a Schimmelpenninck from the top pocket of his suit. He lit it with a gold lighter and looked thoughtful.

'Reason I rang you,' Bobby said. 'I wondered what to make of it.'

'Make of it?'

'Well, is it reasonable? Unusual, yes. Amazing, possibly. And yet I can half see her point of view. Have I the right to deny her the one thing that she's, well, here for?'

'Is this a philosophical discussion?'

'You take a woman's body.'

'A chance would be a fine—'

'The whole damned structure is built exclusively for what we philosophers call propagation. It's not like men. External sex organs, and all that. It's not built into us. We've got more important things to do. Run launderettes.'

'Play snooker.'

'That sort of thing.'

Roland relit his cigar. 'I must say, Robert, that you are taking the most extraordinary attitude to all this. Your wife is indicating that she wants to get screwed by the milkman, and you sit here making droll chat.'

'What attitude would you have me take? I mean, that's the reason I rang you. To discuss it. You think about it. It's not as straightforward as you might imagine. Most people—the fathers of the kids I used to teach—would break their wife's nose at the very suggestion. Or refuse to discuss it—and watch their wives *very* carefully from then on. But where does that lead? One neurotic wife. A marriage wounded, if not broken. What's the good of that?'

'So you want someone to fuck Caroline?'

'I do not.'

'Well, it's beginning to sound like it.'

Bobby finished the lager. He did not know what he wanted. He didn't want anybody to touch Caroline, but he did not want to lose her. He wasn't even sure that he could survive anybody touching her, but he remembered a vow that he had made to himself on the day he got married, that he would not add to the world's total of unhappy wives.

'I don't know,' he said. 'I don't know.' What he had been half hoping was that Roland would come up with another solution, but he knew now that he was wasting his time.

As Roland refilled their glasses, the office-workers began to fill the room with their Christmas parties. This was the day of the year when solicitors laid their secretaries, and unspeakable events took place behind the filing cabinets. A year's repressed sexuality was unleashed on a Yuletide of drink, and next week the inhibitions would be back in place for another frustrating year.

Bobby drank half a pint of lager without stopping.

'Well, what do you think, Hodgson?' he said.

Roland shrugged. 'If what you want is a volunteer, consider me as having taken two paces forward. Greater love hath no man than that he lay his friend's wife when she's down.'

'I don't suppose you're quite what she's got in mind. A Nobel prize-winning Olympic gold medallist might have the necessary qualifications.'

'Mention my offer, anyway. Of course, she'll have to remind me how to do it.'

'I haven't got a Christmas present yet for her. I suppose I could send you gift-wrapped.'

'I've always wanted to be at stud. It's time I had a new money-making idea. Perhaps that's it.'

'You'd cover a few mares in a season, wouldn't you? What's

41

this new barmaid called? I'd buy you a drink if I knew.'

'Heather. Isn't she a pure-looking lady? The trouble is that it's always that sort that want to be manacled to the bedstead and lashed with rubber hoses.'

'Heather,' Bobby said.

The barmaid, a tall, blonde girl with a round face and deep blue eyes, came over to their corner of the counter. Bobby gave her their empty glasses.

'Keep taking the Pils,' she said with a laugh.

Bobby laughed too, but Roland said sternly: 'I'll crack the jokes round here, if you don't mind.'

The room was crowded now and several couples were kissing, not necessarily beneath the mistletoe. 'So this is Christmas,' John Lennon was singing on the jukebox, but his voice could hardly be heard above the festive babble of the bar. Bobby slipped off his stool and went to the gents. There was an addition to the graffiti that he had missed last night: Why are you looking up here? Ashamed of it? And underneath, the reply: Ashamed of it? Just looking at it frightens me to death. But he found that the phallic joke had lost its appeal since the news arrived from Doctor Grimshaw: the emasculation had removed him from certain areas of humour. He was a man with a hidden flaw, like a secret whisky drinker, relentlessly killing himself on the quiet. But it wasn't so serious as secret whisky drinking, nor so deadly. He was more of a secret lemonade drinker, a man with a bizarre but harmless blemish.

Tim Franklin, the local district reporter for the county newspaper, had arrived in the bar when he got back.

'I'm a secret lemonade drinker,' Bobby told him.

Tim Franklin didn't hear. 'How is the dirty knicker business?' he asked. 'Are you getting rich?'

'Yes oblique no,' Bobby said. 'You want a drink?'

'Did you hear that?' said Roland, who was now laughing. 'I asked Heather if she did salmon and cucumber, and she said "Not if I have to get my ankle behind my neck"! She's a bit of a laugh, that girl. I may take her up.'

'You were probably right about her. She does want to be manacled to the bed.'

'Where can I get some rubber hoses, Tim?' Roland asked.

Tim Franklin shrugged. 'What are you alcoholic pair talking

about?' he asked. He was a tall, thin young man, with a red velvet jacket, thick horn-rimmed spectacles and long blond hair. His frequent arrivals in the Planet were not, in Bobby's view, great cause for celebration. In Bobby's view, Tim Franklin over-estimated his own importance, despite the evidence which faced him every day: the trivia with which he was involved. Like all journalists, he was always hoping for the unusual, but found himself surrounded by the tedious. He spent his life waiting for the corpse to start chatting with the mourners, but it never happened, and his solemn conversations were mostly about council meetings, planning inquiries, petitions about trees, storms in thimbles, rows that simmered but did not erupt. The real stories in the town—the bribery and corruption, the councillors with poorly paid jobs who mysteriously drove around in £4,000 cars, the bent scout-masters, absentee MPS, captious magistrates, selective police-men—he was prevented from publishing by the laws of libel. The *Clarion* came out every Friday, full of whist-drive results and speeding fines, and Tim Franklin looked upon it and found it good.

Bobby bought him a lager.

'Tell us all the exciting stuff that's been going on in this town,' he said. 'I hear the vicar farted last week.'

'You tell me the news,' Tim Franklin said. 'I sell it.'

'What you sell, Timothy, is a cure for insomnia. You ought to drop all this man of letters bollocks and come out into the real world and do some work.'

Timothy sipped his lager thoughtfully. Nothing this side of thirty-five was going to dent his self-esteem. 'I don't wish to lay a vast irretrievable slab of my life on the altar of com-merce, thank you. I'm a creative person.'

'What you are creating, old fruit, is a hotbed of fucking apathy,' said Roland. 'When I've made a bit more money I'll buy your paper up, then we'll make the town jump.'

The bar was so full now that it was difficult to move. People had stopped talking and were beginning to shout.

'Caracas has got a fantastic temperature,' said a loud young man behind them.

'I didn't even know he was ill,' Roland told him. 'Heather, darling, put a few whiskies on this part of the counter, and I'll let you come to my party tonight.'

'Give me a bucket of sand and I'll do the bloody desert song,' she said gaily.

'You poor over-worked thing. Forget that rabble. You've got cash customers here. You'll get your reward tonight.'

The drinks appeared and disappeared. Somebody started to sing a carol.

'Oh, sparkling event, where are you?' Roland said, peering round the bar. 'I find it so hard to have hope in this weather.'

Bobby felt the warm whisky go down and began to forget why he had come into the Planet. Then he had another and remembered that he had still to buy a Christmas present for Caroline. If he stayed in here much longer, this Christmas was going to slip past in a haze. He stood up and felt drunk.

'Got to buy a Christmas present,' he said. 'Thank you for your useless advice.'

He found himself in the street after a long struggle with the revellers. In the square, the carol-singers were grouped round the Christmas tree, but on the pavements at the side the rattling of the charity collectors' money-boxes was louder than the singing. Bobby ignored both and walked slowly up the street looking in the shop windows for Christmas present ideas. These days it was difficult to find the real shops among the building societies, estate agents, betting shops and travel firms, but he eventually reached a jewellers, and saw a gold bracelet in the window for £62. The small Jewish manager recoiled from his alcoholic fumes, but accepted his cheque.

'Generous is the word that will be mumbled tearfully as the sombre thousands file past my catafalque,' he told the manager solemnly. Saying it, he realised that he was drunk. He could get plastered at lunch time on half the quantity it took at night.

He put the parcel in his pocket and headed across the square to the launderette: he hadn't put an armchair in his office for nothing. The carol-singers were making a pretty hefty din now with 'Silent Night', and he might have to tone it down a little. Chap here trying to get some sleep.

Not surprisingly, the shop was empty. He went straight through to his office and slumped drunkenly in his chair. What he wanted to do was collect his thoughts on the domestic débâcle which confronted him, but the alcohol had anaesthetised his head.

In a relationship with a woman, did anything ever match the first sweet moments? He remembered the day that she had arrived in his classroom, armed with questionnaires, notebooks and charts. He could not reconcile her beauty with her efficiency: it was not a combination that he had found sitting side by side before.

'It's awfully good of you to let me interrupt your class like this,' she said, as the children filled in her questionnaire. Her voice was deeper than most women's and highly provocative.

'I want to marry you,' he was going to say and would have said except that the remark would be picked up like radar by the big ears in the front row. 'What are you doing exactly?' he asked instead.

Caroline smiled a little apology. 'The magazine is doing a big series on Today's Children. How bright they are. What they think. Their ambitions. How they compare with kids of the same age twenty, thirty years ago. My bit of it is the twelve-year-olds. I'd like to talk to a few of them afterwards when they've filled in the form.'

'Use my desk.'

An hour later, equipped with the most up-to-date information on the thinking of twelve-year-old children today, her job was done.

'I'm in your debt,' she said politely, as the class filed out.

It was such a happy choice of words that he wondered whether she could see the invitation looming.

'It's easily paid,' he said, gathering up his copies of Ridout's *English Today*. 'That building you see through that window over there is one of those public house places. You give the man money, he gives you drinks.'

'I'll buy you one,' said Caroline. 'Are those your own teeth?'

He looked down into her grey eyes and realised triumphantly that he was pushing at an open door.

He remembered that first evening in the pub, five hours that lasted five minutes, dining at the bar on Camembert and celery, neither of them wanting to break the spell by moving to a different atmosphere, and Caroline almost missing the last train back to London. There was no question of her staying in his flat: it would have been crass to suggest it. Most relationships today began on the bed and developed or withered from there; but this one wasn't like that. This was *the* girl, and they had all the time that was coming.

'Where shall I meet you in London tomorrow?' he asked as they reached the station.

'Are you meeting me in London tomorrow? How nice of you.'

'I'll be the one with the red roses.'

'And lovely teeth.'

'You've got a thing about molars, Miss Ford.'

'My father is a dentist in Dorchester. Our family fortune is founded on teeth.'

She gave him her card: Caroline Ford, Features Writer. Her office was in the Bayswater Road.

'I'll be there at five o'clock,' he told her. 'No cheese and celery tomorrow.'

He watched her climb into the train: brown thighs from a white mini-skirt.

The following mid-summer afternoon, armed incredibly with a dozen red roses, he arrived at her office in London. She took the flowers and he took her hand.

'I've decided to marry you,' he said.

'What took you so long to make up your mind, Bobby?' she answered. 'I can't stand indecisive men.'

'The school holidays start next month.'

She kissed him on the cheek: their first kiss. 'I'll give in my notice tomorrow,' she said. 'Now you can take me to my favourite French restaurant.'

He remembered all that. It was more like a story out of her magazine than real life.

He remembered standing on the tarmac at Heathrow (wondering idly why the word QUIM was printed quite so prominently on the cover of British passports) and trying to locate and identify the new pressures of responsibility that his just-acquired marital status imposed.

Mummy and Daddy had driven up from Piddletrenthide, near Dorchester, for twenty minutes in the Register Office and three hours of Lanson Black Label champagne in a private

46

room at the local three-star hotel, before taking them to the airport for a final, tearful farewell with their lovely girl.

Bobby had rather liked them, which seemed almost unnatural, a certain amount of internecine strife with the in-laws being part of the nuts and bolts of modern marriage. Even more surprisingly—Caroline being an only child, and Bobby being an impoverished, ageing school-teacher turned launderette manager—they seemed to like him.

Mrs Ford took him on one side after a few glasses of champagne to give him a brief run-down on lovely Caroline's fun-packed twenty-five years. Like most mothers of an only child, Mrs Ford, a tall well-preserved woman in her late forties, clearly believed that every stage of Caroline's development had been remarkable, from the time that she learned to read at four. It was equally clear that she loved to talk about it, to share it with the world, and to dwell, lengthily if possible, on the triumphs along the way, the exams that were easily passed and the admirers who had always hovered—poor inferior creatures—in the background. But she had never been so fortunate in her audience. She talked in a prim and prissy way that somehow managed to convey the impression that she was knitting with her teeth, but Bobby listened in pure delight : he thought Caroline was remarkable, too.

Mr Ford, medium height, grey hair, worn but handsome face, leapt most unexpectedly into Bobby's pantheon of heroes. He asked what time they had to be at the airport, and said that although he had travelled thousands of miles by sea, he had never flown. Bobby asked him about the sea, and Mr Ford told him about his war. He had joined the Navy at eighteen and was immediately assigned to the Russian convoys. The temperature for most of the time was below freezing point, and they couldn't wash or change their clothes. They were in the dark because lights were dangerous, and spent most of the time knee-deep in icy water, working below deck. If this is life, let's get torpedoed, he thought one evening, and the idea evidently appealed to somebody because the torpedo hit them that night. Four survived two days on a raft; forty-seven were already dead.

It sounded like the sort of experience that would have haunted Bobby, but it didn't seem to mean much to Mr Ford.

At the end of the war, the government gave him a grant to go to dental college.

Bobby shook his hand at the airport, and kissed his mother-in-law's cheek.

'She's all yours now,' said Mrs Ford, with a large smile.

'Aren't I lucky?' said Bobby.

They flew off into more sun. Sussex lay beneath them.

'Nice parents you've got, Mrs Booth.'

'Mummy goes on a bit, though, doesn't she? I saw her button-hole you.'

'She was giving me the goods on you.'

'I bet she was. Donkeys hang on to their hind legs when she gets going.'

He laughed at his clever bride. They both laughed for most of the week, a week of sangria, sunshine and sex. They made love every few hours. Caroline was astonished by his virility. She didn't know that he had been saving up for two years. He found her so exciting that it was no trouble at all to start all over again. He was enslaved by the contours of her breasts.

They looked round the shops in the morning, lay on the beach in the afternoon, and went to clubs, barbecues or bars until the early hours of the morning; and they always held hands.

He remembered it all. But what he remembered best now was their last evening at a Danish restaurant on the Via Roma after they had watched El Cordobes' second bull lie down and refuse to get up.

'I want to have four children,' Caroline had said. 'You miss a lot being an only child.'

'Four? Really?'

She did not have the pale, anxious-to-please face of an insecure young wife, and she never would have.

'Four. Quite definitely. You'd better have some more steak.'

When he woke up it was dark. He looked at his watch: six o'clock. His head had partially cleared, but he was starving. He hadn't eaten since breakfast. He stood up and lit a cigarette. He would shut up the shop, walk briskly home, have a shower and a meal, and then take Caroline off to Roland's party where the Christmas fun would really begin.

As he got to the door of his office, a familiar shape came into

48

the shop from the street. She walked down to the detergent dispenser, put in five pence, caught the little round packet as it shot out of the machine, and went over to one of the washing machines. She was the only person in the shop. And she had no washing.

Bobby, still muzzy after his drunken sleep, noticed this last fact while pretending not to watch her. She was still asking how we can lose when we're so sincere, but her Christmas card of this morning had filled him with alarm signals, and he stayed well back. He could not take his eyes off her, though. From his angle she seemed to be all breasts and buttocks.

She produced some change from the pockets of her jeans and put it in the washing machine. Then she turned the control dial from warm to hot. What happened after that became inscribed on his mind so that years afterwards he could order an action replay in his head.

Crossing her arms suddenly, with her right hand on her left hip and her left hand on her right hip, she pulled the yellow T-shirt over her head, pushed it into the washing machine and dropped the lid. She pushed the coin tray to start the machine and then stood back, naked from the waist up, as if this sort of thing went on all the time.

Bobby, transfixed by her shape, stood staring from the door of his office. But beyond the girl was the street and the shoppers—who were still hurrying somewhere, chasing the last box of crackers or the last loaf of bread—and any minute now a friendly policeman would go wandering by. Launderette manager in orgy shock.

He stepped out of his office and the girl turned to face him.

'Hallo,' she said. 'I guessed you were in there.'

'Nice to see you,' he said jokily. 'But don't you think you had better wait in my office?'

'I do. I do,' said the girl. 'That's just what I think.' She walked passed him with a smile. 'I was going to ask you if I could wait in here. You see, I want to wash these as well.'

Before Bobby could assemble a reply, the girl was sliding her jeans down over her thighs. She stepped out of them neatly and handed them to him.

'Perhaps you'd better put them in the machine,' she said. 'Let me just empty the pockets.' She took out some money and a Zippo and handed him back the jeans. But as he turned to go, she started to pull her panties down as well. 'You might as well do these at the same time,' she said, smiling.

He did not trust himself to speak. He put his cigarette in the ashtray on his desk, took the clothes into the shop and put them into the washing machine. Then he conducted a few tests, digging nails into his hands and face, to see whether he had woken up or whether this was all part of the post-Planet dream, but came up with no answer. Presumably you could dream that you dug your nails into your face.

He walked quickly to the shop door, locked it and flicked the OPEN sign to CLOSED. Then he took a long breath and returned to his office. The girl was sitting on the end of his desk like a nude model in a magazine. He found that he was standing very close to her.

'We don't get a lot of naked girls in here,' he said, reaching past her for his cigarette. Her body was remarkable. He could see that a pencil placed beneath her breasts would fall straight to the floor and the pubic hair area seemed to be about the size of Wembley Stadium. His body liked it, too.

'Did you get my Christmas card?' she asked.

'I couldn't send one back. I didn't know your address. Or your name.'

'Josie,' said the girl. 'Your name is Bobby.'

'I know. But how did you?'

'I've seen you around.'

'Are you an art student?'

'Among other things.'

He went round and sat down at his desk to remove the temptations that were emerging.

'Well, it's certainly nice to see you, Josie. What else do you do?'

'I fuck.'

'Very good for the muscles, that. I meant what else do you do apart from being an art student?'

'I model for the life classes.'

'In the nude?'

'Of course.'

'I thought you seemed pretty relaxed with no clothes on.'

She stood up and walked round to his chair.

50

'Would you like to touch them?' she said. She was leaning forward so that her breasts hovered before his face. The next thing he knew was that her nipple was in his mouth and his hands were gripping her bottom. Then her hand was in his trousers and he was on the floor. Then she was on top of him, her breasts pressed into his face. Then he was on top of her. He lay there afterwards staring into the carpet from a distance of about two inches.

'The washing machine has stopped,' he said, hauling himself on to his elbows.

'So have you,' said Josie. 'Can I put some more money in?' Her black hair was spread over the carpet as she smiled up at him.

He eased himself up slowly. 'I'll put your clothes in the drier. Have it on the house.'

'One good tumble deserves another,' said Josie. She made no effort to get up.

Bobby went out and transferred the clothes. He felt empty and depressed. He had never been unfaithful to Caroline before. When he returned to his office, Josie was sitting in his chair.

'You came here to do that, didn't you?'

'Oh yes.'

'Why?'

'I fancied you, of course. Have you any cigarettes? I'm out.'

He gave her a Silk Cut and lit it for her. She blew the smoke at the ceiling. He watched her but could find nothing to say.

After a while, she asked: 'Do you get many one-legged men in here?'

'We get the odd naked lady.'

'You have a box full of socks out there and a notice saying, "Match your odd socks from here." '

'Actually, all the people who come in here have got more than the average number of legs.'

'How's that?'

'Have you ever seen anyone with three legs?'

'Only you just now.'

'Plenty of people with one leg, though. So the average number of legs among human beings must be less than two, mustn't it?'

'Very clever.' She gave him a sidelong glance. 'Are you married?'

Bobby looked at her and nodded. She had a pleasant face with wide-apart eyes. He hadn't noticed her face before.

'How draggy,' she said. 'Any children?'

Outside, he could hear, the rain had started again.

'No,' he answered. 'No children.'

At midnight he was sitting on the floor with a Lloyds' San Toy cheroot in one hand and a half pint mug of champagne in the other. He had tried standing up but after a while had almost felt what little vitality he had left draining away through his feet. From the floor everything seemed a lot cosier.

Rotund Roland threw a party when he was uncertain where the next bout of sex was coming from: the party asked the question and, usually, answered it. The parties that he threw were several cuts above most that Bobby had got drunk at. There were no tins of beer, no four-pint cans of some unspecified brown stuff, no supermarket plonk. The crates of champagne never ran out, and nor did the whisky, gin, vodka, bacardi, tequila, brandy or rum.

Roland's third house in three years was a Georgian mansion standing in an acre of ground on the outskirts of the town. It was surrounded by many trees, and tucked away in various parts of his acre were a double-garage, an empty barn, an orchard, a derelict and empty swimming-pool, and a hard tennis court that was gradually going to grass. Inside there were a maze of rooms, most of them little used and consequently sparsely furnished.

Up to a hundred people were now milling around, from one room to another, searching for something as party guests always are. One room had been turned into a bar where Heather was opening bottles of champagne at the rate of one a minute. In another, darker, room people were dancing or just moving slightly to a tape of recent hit records.

Bobby was sitting on the floor alone in a third room. There were other people around, but they were nothing to do with him. He must have been to a thousand parties in his life—the party was the native fertility dance of the Western world—but he had not enjoyed many of them. In the old days they were a

52

flesh hunt—except for a serious young man he had known in his teens who was preparing himself for Oxford and did not intend to be lumbered with any emotional luggage until certain academic targets had been reached. He used to masturbate before every party and then get happily stoned in the kitchen, ruthlessly immune to the blandishments of angel-faced schoolgirls.

Nowadays, married man Bobby found that parties were not the same. He was expected to sip wine and politely exchange opinions with businessmen who thought Hitler was dangerously left-wing, or trade unions were a Communist conspiracy, or the gallows must be swiftly re-built if civilisation was to survive on these embattled shores. Or just with good old middle-class bank clerks, and salesmen, and accountants, most of them pretentious to a degree that numbed the mind.

Was this really true he wondered. Or had recent events inserted a new misanthropic streak into his disintegrating personality? He put on his rose-coloured spectacles to study the guests.

There was a short, fat man called Bill Fortescue, age fifty-three, who liked to be known as Colonel Fortescue. He had since the war been the local Conservative Party agent, a desk-bound sinecure which had given him status, influence, three chins and piles down to his knee-caps. He went in for brown tweed three-piece suits, and his silver hair was always immaculately brushed back so that he looked just like the character he was supposed to be playing. The Member of Parliament whose interests he protected had a 22,000 majority. What protection did a 22,000 majority need? Bill Fortescue filled in the time by talking to any group of people who invited him, so long as they threw in dinner, and perfecting his snooker in the Conservative Club. Virtues? He had a habit of talking with his eyes closed, which relieved the listener of the necessity to feign interest, no small bonus where Bill Fortescue was concerned.

There was Steve Sinclair and his wife Lynn. Steve Sinclair was one of Roland's friends from his more recent money-making period, a period which had opened a few doors that Bobby would have preferred to remain closed. Steve was twenty-five, tall and good-looking, the only son of a wealthy estate agent whose vast and finagling empire he would one day inherit. He had big brown eyes and a meaty, open-pored type of face which women found earthy, attractive. His voice began conversations at a conventional volume but increased to a bray under pressure, and his laugh, which acknowledged his own remarks more often than other people's, was half-way between a machine-gun volley and a death rattle. His small, pale wife had been a beautiful bride at nineteen, but six years of blissful domesticity had changed all that. She gave Bobby the impression that in some area of her marriage she had taken on more than she could handle, but was going to hang on now for dear life. To see someone so young look so harassed was fascinating, like a car accident.

There was landlord Basil, fresh from a hectic night in the Planet, who, Bobby could hear, was telling creative newshound Tim Franklin what wonderful stereo equipment Roland had. There was a shy, swarthy young man called Rodney, whom Bobby had seen around for as long as he could remember. Rodney stood on the edge of a conversation but nobody spoke to him, so he blew perfect smoke rings into the air but nobody noticed. He was the man who always stepped out of the way on the pavement, the man who looked guilty when it was somebody else who had farted. When Roland told him one drunken evening in the Planet that if all Englishmen were like him we wouldn't have colonised the Ise of Wight yet, he had nodded his agreement.

In among the married couples who were sipping champagne and discussing the rising cost of Christmas, was Darryl Blundell, the only convicted villain on the guest list. Darryl had recently emerged from a six-month stay in prison for theft—he had blown himself up trying to rob a gas meter—and was promising everybody that he was a new man. At the moment he was drawing the dole from the Labour Exchange, having assured them that he was a camel-trainer and defied them to find him a job. He augmented it by buying and selling. Two weeks earlier, while drunk in the Planet, he had bought a donkey for £11, but later in the day, when he had sobered up, he sold it for £15. Despite the odd coup like this, he liked to describe himself as the only poor Jew in town.

Bobby watched Darryl, a small, fleshy man of thirty who

looked like forty, and decided to join him. At least you knew where you were with Darryl. It was typical of Roland to invite him to a party like this, and then enjoy the shock or embarrassment when Darryl revealed that he had just come out of prison.

'Found anything worth nicking?' Bobby asked.

Darryl made a V-sign.

'There are some sorts here, aren't there?' he said. 'Why are women so lovely when men are so horrible?'

The thought had probably originated in prison.

'In the animal world it's the other way around,' Bobby said. 'It's the male who is more attractive.'

'That's why there are more people than animals. Have you seen that new barmaid from the Planet? Brings a lump to your trousers.'

'Let's go and get some champagne from her.'

'Good thinking, Carruthers.'

Bobby liked champagne. In the days when such things seemed to matter, he discovered that five hours of conscientious champagne-drinking killed the premature ejaculation stone dead. After five hours of champagne drinking, an orgasm before breakfast was a premature ejaculation.

A group of people were singing 'Mary's Boy Child' in the bar. A man with a white face and no shoulders was kissing the cheeks of every woman within reach.

'It's midnight,' somebody shouted. 'It's Christmas Day!'

They pushed their way through to where Heather was still pouring champagne. Caroline was talking to Roland.

'Does your wife get her bras from rent-a-hammock?' Darryl asked.

'Hallo darling,' said Caroline to Bobby. 'Happy Christmas! Where have you been?'

She looked up to be kissed and he kissed her.

'Happy Christmas to you,' he said. She was wearing an ankle-length blue dress that revealed as much at the top as it concealed at the bottom. He could not remember her ever wearing it before but had learned enough not to mention the fact: she had probably worn it the previous week.

'I've been circulating,' he said. 'Spreading myself around a bit, sharing my wit with the masses.'

'He's been sitting in a corner looking miserable,' Darryl said.

'Well, I'm a secret lemonade drinker,' Bobby said. 'Have you met my friend Darryl Blundell, darling? The internationally famous lateral thinker.'

'He works for the gas board,' Roland said. 'No brains but all the social graces.'

Caroline smiled at Darryl. 'Are you one of the disreputable bunch from the Planet?'

'Star of stage, screen and magistrates' court,' said Roland. 'How are you, Darryl, old fruit? Get yourself some champagne.'

Bobby put his arm round Caroline's shoulder. 'Has Mr Hodgson been looking after you?' he asked.

'She's been telling me what a wonderful husband she has,' said Roland. 'I keep telling her you're a no-good ratbag, but it's an uphill struggle.'

Bobby was intensely curious about what their conversation had really included, and he said nothing. Had they been discussing The Problem?

He lit a cheroot. Cancer cures smoking.

'If I were a carpenter and you were a lady would you get 'em off?' Roland asked.

Caroline was flirty with the drink. 'Don't excite me, Roland. I'm a cauldron of passion.'

'Remember the tenth commandment, fatty,' said Bobby. 'Thou shalt not covet thy neighbour's ass.'

'Your wife after some self-denial award, Bobby?' He tried a musical belch by way of comment.

'Don't belch in front of my wife, Hodgson.'

'I'm terribly sorry. I didn't realise it was her turn. The old jokes are the best,' he said as they all laughed.

Roland had really dressed up for the party, Bobby noticed. White silk shirt, gold cufflinks, immaculate striped tie, charcoal grey suit and hand-stitched shoes. He also thought that he was beginning to see in Roland's eyes the lonely, wistful look that some bachelors developed after a few drinks.

'I used to have the women swooning at my feet,' Roland said, looking round the room.

'But now he washes them,' Bobby told Caroline. Everybody laughed.

56

He thrust his empty glass in Heather's direction. She flicked back her long blonde hair and poured his champagne. On the wall behind her, a poster said: Today is the first day in the rest of your life.

'You just can't stop serving drinks, can you?' he said.

'Ah, but I don't have to add up here,' she said. 'Is Roland married or anything?'

The question took him mildly by surprise. 'Roland? The man with atrophied Jenny Taylor? Certainly not.'

Her blue eyes frowned. 'Is he queer?'

'Why? Are you after his body?' She gave him a look which was meant to convey something, but he couldn't get the message. Perhaps Roland's luck was about to change.

He turned to see that the world celibacy quarter-finalist was still talking to his wife. Until today he had always believed that Roland regarded Caroline as a beautiful but cool young lady who wasn't his type. Since he had heard that Caroline wanted a baby he had begun to show a lot more interest, even to the extent of ignoring a hundred other guests.

He went over to them.

'Heather is after your body,' he said. 'At least, I think she is. Given average luck and a following wind, you could get your leg over there, fatty.'

'Elegant, your husband,' Roland said. 'Nice turn of phrase.'

'Unnecessarily circumlocutory, I thought,' Caroline said.

'My wife's a journalist, you see. Pares sentences to the bone. Wouldn't know an adjective if it bit her on the nose. Do you mind if I borrow her? I feel the urge to dance.'

He took Caroline's hand and led her through to the next room. Dancing with her in the dark, it came back to him suddenly, like a wave of nausea, that he had been unfaithful to her that afternoon. It was something that he had never expected to happen because all his sexual impulses had been focused on her from the first day. The idea that an unknown woman had wandered into his life and seduced (raped?) him on the floor of his office was already unreal, and he had to think hard to convince himself that it had really happened. When it became real again, he set about justifying his behaviour, for his own peace of mind. He had always been good at that.

He had been testing himself, he decided, and it was a vital

57

test that he had passed. If you let a man know that he is sterile, he had read somewhere, you can do him so much psychological damage that it is often better that he is not told. Even quite intelligent men confuse fertility with virility, and it can destroy their sex lives. Some turn to homosexuality; others never have an erection again. He knew all this, and it made the strange events of the afternoon understandable, even necessary. The other much simpler explanation, that he was sex-starved and drunk when a beautiful woman thrust her naked body in his face, did not match the enormity of his offence.

He held Caroline very close.

'What's Roland been on about?' he asked.

'Nothing in particular. He seems awfully friendly tonight.'

He buried his cheek in her hair. It smelled of roses. 'That's what I thought.'

'Does he know?'

'Yes.'

So they hadn't been discussing it.

'You shouldn't have told him.'

Bobby didn't say anything.

'Perhaps he is going to offer his services,' Caroline whispered.

They bumped into people in the dark. An old Manfred Mann number filled the room.

Steve Sinclair, the estate agent, appeared through the gloom. 'Hallo, Bobby. I must have a dance with your ravishing wife.'

'I should ask her first,' Bobby said.

Suddenly the two of them had drifted off into the hot darkness leaving Bobby at the edge of the room. He headed for the door and found Lynn Sinclair trying to monitor her husband's movements.

'He's taken my wife,' Bobby said lightly.

'It's no compliment. He'd take anybody's wife.'

He decided to avoid any biting revelations on the Sinclairs' domestic situation that might be hovering bitterly on Mrs Sinclair's lips, and pressed through to the bar again where he had two very quick glasses of champagne. Roland was now engrossed with Heather, and Tim Franklin, the reporter, was explaining to a toothy girl that young ladies stopped riding horses when they had an adequate sex life.

People were beginning to sit down now under the weight of the champagne. Others, who had children, were heading for home to transfer secret hoards of toys into pillow-cases. A few were arriving, uplifted by their once-a-year visit to church for midnight mass, or perhaps with their appetites whetted by the communion wine.

It was time to find the loo. Booth's law stated that the amount of time you spent drinking without going to the loo, you would subsequently spend going to the loo without drinking. On that form he would be up all night.

The Hodgson bathroom had been rebuilt to Roland's specifications. At the centre of it was a blue double-bath where sexual excitement and hygiene were scheduled to meet among the bubbles. So far it had not happened. Bobby remembered the huge circular bed and black sheets that Roland had bought at the same time, confident that his private life was about to enter a new busy phase. Sadly, his sex life had collapsed at the very moment that he had made these investments.

Bobby, bored, timed himself at the loo. One minute, forty-five seconds. Nearly an English native and British all-comers' record. A trifle more bladder control and he would be pissing for Britain. He threw some water over his face at the sink, and decided that it was time to stop moping nervously about what, if anything, his wife was planning, and get a grip on the party.

A few mental adjustments and he was a new man.

One o'clock found him explaining to the Conservative agent why he could not count on Bobby's support the next time the votes were counted.

'If we all had exactly the same chance, I'd be a Tory,' he announced between gulps of champagne. 'If we all began from the same starting line, the Conservative philosophy would be the only correct one. It would have to be.'

'It is,' said Bill Fortescue mildly.

'You take two babies both born tonight,' said Bobby. If anybody wanted to talk now they could not depend on his listening. 'Two babies. If where they are going to get to in the next forty years was entirely up to them, up to their efforts, I'd vote for your lot. But if one is the son of Lord Fartface, and his name is down for Eton, and the other is the son of a seventeen-year-old unmarried factory girl, the second one has had it before it starts.'

Bill Fortescue was trying to disagree with some of this, but Bobby didn't notice.

'Not only that,' he said. 'The second one has pretty well had it even before he's born. Heredity, genes, all that. If you took the two of them away from their parents tomorrow, and brought them up in the same environment somewhere else, Lord Fartface's son would still be a lap ahead by the time they were seven.'

A young man who had stopped alongside them, attracted by Bobby's evangelical tone, said: 'Who was it who said that Conservatism is a programme for thugs carried out by gentlemen, and Socialism is a programme for gentlemen carried out by thugs?'

'It certainly wasn't me,' said Bobby.

Roland appeared with his arm round Heather. 'What sort of conversation is this?' he asked. 'A white rabbit wearing a wrist-watch is going to dash past in a minute.'

'Where's my wife?' said Bobby. 'I've definitely got a wife somewhere.'

'She's dancing with that nice Mr Sinclair. Such a personable young man.'

'What—still? Mr Sinclair seems to have stumbled across a fool-proof method of getting his teeth loosened.'

When he got back to the room where the dancing was, Lynn Sinclair was still at the door.

'They're kissing,' she said. She had greedy little eyes and a slack mouth, he noticed. Champagne made you observant like that. He pushed through the bodies, but could hardly see in the dark. Then he saw them in the middle of the room. He went over.

'It's my turn, I think.'

They stopped kissing.

'Hallo Bobby,' said Caroline.

'Oh, do piss off,' said Steve Sinclair, and tried to continue with the kissing.

Bobby put his left hand on Sinclair's right arm, pulled it away from his body to open the target, and hit him in the solar plexus with his right fist, turning his body with the punch. Sinclair doubled up and hit the floor, twitching, unable to catch his breath.

Caroline stared, unbelievingly. 'That's disgraceful,' she said.

'Come on,' Bobby said. 'You're drunk.'

'I'm not drunk. It's Christmas.'

He took her firmly by the arm and led her back into the room that he had just left. Roland watched them come in.

'You've found her,' he said.

'He's just hit Steve,' Caroline said. 'Do you allow your guests to behave like that?'

'Did you really hit him? What happened?'

'He wouldn't let go of her. Told me to piss off. I'm afraid my wife is a little drunk. She's not used to all this champagne.'

'I've never known him hit anyone before,' Caroline said, shaking her head. 'I can't stand violence.'

'What happened when you hit him?' Heather asked. 'Did he go down?'

'For ten,' said Bobby. 'You don't mind violence do you?' The incident had exhilarated him, got rid of some tension.

'I love it,' said Heather laughing.

'I think we should go home,' said Caroline. 'Bobby's spoilt everything.'

Bobby was polite. 'I'll get your coat, darling. We'll walk home in the fresh air and sober you up.'

He found her coat, a short white fur coat that looked expensive but wasn't, and when he returned she was still apologising to Roland.

'There is nothing to apologise for, dear,' he said. He had his arm round Heather, and Bobby thought that he would probably be quite happy if everybody else went home, too.

Outside it was cold but the clouds had floated away and the sky was a ceiling of stars. Caroline walked briskly, in silence.

'Cheer up, lovely,' Bobby said. 'It's Christmas.' He did his Gene Kelly act on the edge of the pavement.

'Christmas comes but once a year
And when it does it's bloody dear,'

61

he sang.

But she would not be lured. 'I just can't get over you behaving like that,' she said. 'He's such a pleasant man.'

Bobby stopped dancing. He had been nervously watching Roland all evening. Was the challenge really to come from Steve Sinclair?

'Pleasant? Jesus! He's vain. He's loud. He's spoilt. He's ignorant. There's no brain in that head, you know. He's just an overpaid barrel of lard walking on people's faces.'

Caroline walked quickly, and he had to hurry to stay with her.

'Wherever did this aggressive new streak come from anyway?' she said, looking straight ahead.

He had never seen her so angry. 'It arrived shortly after the appearance of your new flirtatious streak,' he said.

'One boozy Christmas kiss . . .'

He had no answer. But after the last twenty-four hours, one boozy Christmas kiss was a kick in the groin of the marriage that he was now desperately anxious to preserve. He was beginning to see visions of it ending, and he did not like them. He had been a late convert to marriage and, like all late converts, he was not amenable to reason: his enthusiasm was total, even aggressive.

In the days when he proudly deluded himself that it was only his uniquely agile footwork and a God-given sixth sense that had kept him safely clear of matrimony's jail, he could not have imagined how pointless, even desolate, his bachelor's dance was going to appear in retrospect, once Caroline had drifted magically into his life to bring it substance and purpose.

Tonight, with his mounting paranoia feeding on the champagne, the wet smack of a Christmas kiss was indistinguishable from the sound of his marriage fracturing.

THREE

It was a Christmas to forget and, by the time the new year had arrived with its unwanted gift of snow, he had. The year had been given a cautious welcome at a country club in the heart of Hampshire, but Bobby had passed up the normal joys of New Year resolution making. The outlook, he decided, was murky enough without any self-imposed restraints or impossibly glittering targets receding frustratingly before him.

Roland took Heather who danced all night with an eager queue of young men. Dancing was a sex substitute, and Roland regarded her gyrations gloomily.

'When you dance with young men nowadays they'll be talking about rock music, or their boring motor cars, but they've always got the most enormous hard-on,' she said. 'Say what you like about the young blood—it's certainly enthusiastic.'

The remark made them feel old. The arrival of a new year wasn't necessarily cause for celebration. In three months Bobby would be thirty-three which was as far as the crucified carpenter got, at any rate on this side of the clouds. Was he already approaching that age when a man's nerve began to grow ragged, when fears outnumbered hopes, when hypochondria was rampant and prospects became less interesting than reminiscence?

Two weeks later he came down for an early breakfast while Caroline slept on upstairs. Roland wanted Bobby to join him on a search for shop premises. Expansion was in the air. He left two fried eggs flapping round the edges and wandered into the living-room to find his cigarettes. The week's problems for Susan Smith were piled neatly alongside Caroline's typewriter. He picked them all up and took them through to the kitchen for some light breakfast reading. He scooped out his eggs and sat down.

Dear Susan Smith: I am very worried about my daughter of seventeen who is our only child. Now that she is developing into a beautiful woman she seems to take a delight in walking about the house with very few clothes on. Last week, after a bath, she came into the room where my husband and I were watching television with her blouse undone and nothing underneath so that her father could see her breasts. When I talked to her about it afterwards, she only laughed and said that we are her parents, as if that made it all right. But I don't like the way that my husband is beginning to look at her and I am frightened of what might happen.

Bobby found this much better early-morning reading than Premier Hits Out and he turned to the second problem. A more muscular branch of the magazine business dealt with the really important sexual dilemmas of our time—the men who made love to vacuum cleaners, the women who got satisfaction from their dogs—but Susan Smith still had half the market.

Dear Susan Smith: I am eighteen years old and am going out with my first boyfriend whom I love very much. We have been making love ever since we first met a year ago, but this no longer seems to satisfy him. Sometimes he does it up my bottom although I ask him not to, and he wants me to use my mouth. Should I give him up?

You would never guess all this stuff from looking at people's faces in the street: if all the sexual energy that was simmering out there—from the cheerful lady of the night to the lonely monk, wanking neurotically into his unresponsive cowl—could be harnessed to the national grid, the lights need never go out.
He picked up the third cry for help with a smile of anticipation, but the smile vanished when he saw the address.

Dear Susan Smith: My husband has fallen in love with another woman and is determined to go to bed with her. She is already married, and her husband and my husband had a fight at a Christmas party which has strengthened his determination to take the woman to bed. I think he sees it as revenge. He talks about it quite openly to me because he knows that I will never leave him, and, in a way, feel lucky to have married him. He says that he will never leave me but I am scared that he might prefer her.

He read the letter again, pushed his breakfast aside, and lit a cigarette. It could have been worse, he decided. There were no reports of love from the other man's wife, no requests for babies from wives with sterile husbands. He read through Lynn Sinclair's childish handwriting once more, then piled up the letters in the order that they had been in and replaced them by the typewriter in the next room. Some action seemed to be required from him at this stage, but he wasn't very strong on action this early in the morning. He stood in the middle of the room, his cigarette in his teeth, and reached a decision: he would, in the first place, wait until Caroline had read the letter and see if she showed it to him. If she had nothing to hide, she would; then the subject could be quickly forgotten – just as soon, in fact, as he had broken Steve Sinclair's nose.

He left the house feeling surprisingly buoyant. Sometimes he does it up my bottom! Things were never so bad that somebody couldn't give you a laugh.

Outside, the snow had gone and a bright, heatless sun was sitting idly in the sky.

Roland had an office over a wine shop in one of the town's sidestreets. He had taken it on a long lease during a more active period in his business career, and he kept it now while he waited for the next idea to hit him. He retained his secretary, Della, for the same reason. A plaque on the door outside, made out of plastic but looking like pure gold, said: Roland Hodgson Enterprises.

'And where is the enterprising Mr Hodgson?' Bobby asked as he walked in.

Della was a pale lady of about thirty, slightly overweight from sitting around for too many years and doing nothing. She was reading that week's issue of the magazine that published Susan Smith.

'He's meeting you here ten minutes ago, Bobby,' she said. 'Take a seat.'

But before he could sit down, Roland bounced in.

'Morning, wage slaves,' he said. 'Guess what—I've bought a new car.'

'I hope the firm can afford it,' said Della, putting down her magazine.

'What the firm couldn't afford was my Bentley. I came out of a part-exchange deal with a thousand pounds. Come on Robert, we're going to Alford. Della, phone every estate agent within twenty miles and ask them to send us details of vacant shop premises. Single shops, not bloody supermarkets. Then write to the firms who quoted us prices for washing machines and driers two years ago and ask them what their prices are now.'

'Isn't he brisk?' said Bobby.

He followed Roland downstairs. A metallic blue BMW stood at the kerb. Roland got in and opened the passenger door. Inside it was all luxury.

'Did you ever have Della?' Bobby asked as they drove off. 'She's got a right sinecure there. She must do something for you.'

Roland laughed so that his glasses shook. 'Della? You're joking. She used to be bloody busy, and she will be again when I can figure out what to do.' He eased his new car round the square. 'Another woman I never had is Heather, and I'm not going to by the look of it. She only wants me as a companion. She's only turned on sexually by the physical type of men. Funny that. She has fantasies about big brown labourers in sweaty vests. Not attracted to men of her own IQ.' He considered the rejection, shaking his head. 'She's a primitive, is our Heather. She doesn't want any lover of hers taking off his glasses and feeling his way to the bed. If an unwashed ape leapt out of the gutter and fucked her into a trance she'd be so grateful it'd bring a tear to a glass eye. So what chance has a nice, civilised chap like me got, clean finger-nails, sensitive nature, erection like a Californian sequoia? No chance. Bollocks. I may take up sniffing glue.'

'It damages your brain and your liver.'

'You have to pay for your pleasures in this world, old fruit. Bloody Heather. I thought I was away there.'

He stopped at some traffic lights and tapped his steering wheel thoughtfully. 'I wish I'd been a woman. Have it whenever you want. It must be better—look at the transexual busi-

66

ness. Men are getting themselves turned into women at a rate of knots, but how many women are forking out wages to be turned into a poor, exploited man?'

He pulled a cigar from the top pocket of his suit and lit it with his gold lighter. Smoke drifted round the car.

'I'm going broke,' he said.

They were out of the town now and heading for the ten miles of dual carriageway that led to the neighbouring town of Alford.

'This car doesn't look as if you are going broke,' Bobby said. 'Put some music on.'

Roland pushed in a cassette and the Rolling Stones hit them from all sides of the car.

'This car is my first economy measure.'

'Easy Clean's doing all right. I know that for a fact. I work there.'

Roland nodded. 'You're doing a grand job, Robert. But I've got expenses. There's my office, rent, rates. Della's wages. Upkeep of my house which is bloody expensive. Then there's my life-style. Whisky, cigars ...'

'Which keep going out.'

'I don't spend a lot on wild, wild women, granted. But I am beginning to live on my capital and that's disastrous.' He took out his lighter and re-lit his cigar. 'I was once told that a guards officer never re-lit his cigar. I was down to Tom Thumbs before I decided to rebel.'

They were on the dual-carriageway now and out in the country.

'That Triumph seems to feel a certain obligation to stay ahead of me. Let's see what this blue monster can do.'

The horizon was five miles away in any direction and flat fields lay on both sides, empty fields that would be gold with corn in a few months, or fields with black and white cows dotted among the green. Roland changed gear and the car picked up speed dramatically as they swept past the Triumph.

Bobby looked across at the pleasure on his fat friend's face. He had never understood about car-drivers: their vehicles were never as he would have supposed, a convenient method of getting from one place to another; they became embedded at the heart of their psyche, a reinforcement of their personality, a spare organ.

Roland stayed happily in the outside lane to overhaul two fruit lorries and a sports car and then slowed as the road narrowed to a single lane through the village of Oakway, the only sign of human life on the journey. At one time, as a break from the heart-weakening excitement of past participles, Bobby had tried to interest his empty-eyed class in local history. He set up a study project on the history of Oakway and now there was nothing that he didn't know about the place except the name of a single honest rustic who lived there.

'The Normans held this place in 1086,' he told Roland.

'They've got a good pub.'

'The tin highway, used by Phoenicians, from Cornwall to Thanet ran just north of here.'

'It sells Whitbread,' said Roland. 'But it's closed.'

They passed the pub that sold Whitbread and the petrol station and the village stores and the antique shop that seemed to be mandatory in this part of the world, and then they drove past the war memorial which stood in the middle of the street.

'Out of a population of five hundred, they lost thirty men in the First World War and nineteen in the Second.'

The regurgitated history lesson evoked no response, and they regained the dual-carriageway in silence. Roland soon had his new car in the high eighties.

'Can you think of any money-making schemes?' he asked eventually. 'These should be our peak earning years.'

Bobby realised that he had been ignoring Roland's financial worries. Perhaps they were more serious than he imagined.

'My peak earning year is my first in the grave,' he said. 'I'm heavily insured. Christ knows why.'

They cruised passed a coach full of grey heads.

'I'll give you a couple of money-making schemes, just to keep you going,' Bobby said. 'If you send a bill for less than ten pounds to the chief accountant of all the big companies in Britain, and threaten legal action if it's not paid in ten days, the money will roll in. They don't bother to check anything for that amount and they don't want any legal expenses.' He looked over. Roland managed a smile. 'Or you can advertise a Cornish holiday cottage in the posh papers during the winter and take deposits on next summer's business. As long as you haven't got a cottage there's no problem with double booking or even treble booking. Somebody made ten thousand pounds by May with that trick.'

'I was thinking of something legal,' Roland said. 'I need to make a little more money. Ends are not meeting by several million light years. Oh, we'll make a few bob if we open up at Alford, but costs are rising every bloody day. I don't know what to do. As I grow older I know more and more about less and less. I used to have a fresh money-spinning idea every morning. It was there with my erection when I woke up.'

'Well, you still get the erection. Be thankful for small mercies.'

'There's nothing small about it, old fruit. I practically need planning permission to have it in the first place.'

They arrived at Alford laughing. It was a town of one street almost a mile long; all the big chain-stores were there because although at first glance it looked like the end of the world so far as business possibilities were concerned, it had a huge catchment area in the surrounding countryside.

Roland turned off the main street and drove into the council car park behind a supermarket. They got out of the car. A lady L-driver was taking her new Datsun on an impromptu tour of the car park attendant's foot. Oh, merry day.

Roland pulled some papers from the inside pocket of his suit.

'That nice Mr Sinclair has given me the addresses of three available properties,' he said. 'They're all in the High Street.'

'Sinclair's the estate agent, is he?'

'He's our man. We'll go and see him when we've had a look at the premises. Don't hit him, will you? I wish to do business with him.'

Bobby wanted to tell Roland the latest news about Mr and Mrs Sinclair, but he was prevented from doing so. From the very beginning, Caroline had insisted that her Susan Smith role should not become generally known: she guessed the ribald comments it would attract. She also had the far-fetched idea that somebody they knew might one day write to Susan Smith, not realising who she was. Bobby had laughed a lot about this at the time but she had been triumphantly vindicated in this morning's post.

The first empty shop stood between a Chinese take-away business and a bookmaker's. Bobby could immediately visualise himself picking the winners over his chicken chop suey. According to Roland, it had once been the main gents' hairdressers in the town, with a discreet line in superior contraceptives. The friendly barber who owned the business had discovered one morning with abrupt suddenness that men didn't get their hair cut much any more, and women were on the Pill. He was now in charge of trolley distribution at the supermarket.

It was a long shop with an office at the end, bigger than the Easy Clean they already had.

'How many washing machines could we get down that wall?' Roland asked.

Bobby measured. 'Twelve,' he said. 'What's the rent?'

'Forty pounds a week. It's a good site.'

The second shop was a hundred yards away, a smaller premises between a travel agent and the freezer centre. The rent was only £35 a week but there was room for only six washing machines. The third one was too far from any car park to be of use; people with huge bundles of washing were not great walkers. They wandered back through the shoppers to have another look at the first.

'I think Easy Clean is going to expand just here,' Roland said. 'Let's go and see Mr Sinclair.'

The local branch of Sinclair and Crane, Estate Agents, Surveyors, Valuers and Auctioneers, had one of the best positions in Alford, next to Woolworths. The walls of the office were covered with pictures of beautiful houses with vast lawns and, occasionally, swimming-pools : it was clearly an expensive area in which to settle down. A girl rose by a desk at the door when they went in, but Steve Sinclair, who had been thumbing through some papers at the end of the room, stepped forward when he saw who had come in. He found himself in a difficult position. Here was the man who had hit him but here, too, in the same package, was a man who wanted to do business, put money in his pocket. Predictably, his financial instincts triumphed.

'Roland. Bobby,' he said.

'Morning Steve,' Roland said. 'How long can I rent Seventeen, the High Street for?'

'As long as you like.'

'Five years at the same rent?'

'Certainly. Come through to my office.'

They followed him into a small room at the back. The furniture was functional, but the carpet was lush. Bobby didn't speak. He was beginning to wonder how the renting of Number 17 would affect the even pattern of his life. He could see that his duties were about to be doubled, but what about his salary? Was he going to work twice as hard for the same money to keep Hodgson Enterprises solvent? That was the embarrassment of working for a friend. The familiar regrets along with the usual questions about what he was doing working in a launderette anyway, were queueing in the wings, but Sinclair's machine-gun laughter, much in evidence now with a money-making deal all signed up, distracted him. He stared at the object of his dislike and neurotically itemised his equipment: big, brown dog-like eyes; a nose like a cross-section of the moon; thick red lips like a cow's backside. This cachinnating twerp had always been given everything he ever wanted. Now he wanted Bobby's wife. Itching with ammunition that he could not use, Bobby wanted to tell him about his wife's letter to Susan Smith, but to do so would be to betray Caroline. The question was: would Caroline betray him?

Roland was signing documents, studying rates lists, passing over addresses of solicitors. He was happy. Business bored Bobby, but Sinclair, too, was verging on the exultant. Money was something that Sinclair and Crane could not have too much of.

'I must buy you a drink,' he said, standing up. 'You too, Bobby.' When you had fixed a good deal with the organ grinder, you could afford a nod at the monkey.

They walked up the High Street to a dark little public house called The Crown. It had received the Sinclair seal of approval because of the arithmetic of the barmaid's chest. She was a very tall Swedish girl with blonde hair, white trousers and a luteous blouse that was filled to an amazing degree. It was a dingy, one-bar pub, with a fruit machine and a juke box at one end and three stools fixed to the floor at the bar. The landlord, a small, grey-haired man who looked as if many terrible things had happened to him over the years, gave Steve Sinclair a twisted grin.

'Three pints of gloom-chaser, Edward,' Sinclair said, slumping on to an end stool. 'And one for yourself.'

'Disturbing protuberances,' Roland muttered, taking the middle stool. 'For a woman like that to remain at right angles to the ground is in defiance of all known laws of physics.'

'Unbelievable, aren't they?' Steve Sinclair said gulping his beer.

Bobby drank in silence. He was trying to remember what Lynn Sinclair had said in her letter to Susan Smith. My husband has fallen in love with another woman and is determined to go to bed with her? Was that it? Other questions drifted across his mind. What advice would the oracle hand out to Mrs Sinclair? More important, would Caroline show him the letter?

For almost a month now they hadn't made love. Not quite imperceptibly, the space between them had expanded. He could sense it everywhere. At first, he had let it pass—expansion, contraction, the politics of marriage. But the previous night he had got home early for an evening alone with her, an evening not merely to paper over the cracks, but to repair them.

She had been uncharacteristically busy. Susan Smith's problems lay in a pile beside her typewriter, shouting for an answer, but there were ten shirts to be ironed first, a skirt to be altered, a new book about the Russian convoys to be parcelled up as a present for her father, an accompanying letter to be written, the washing up to be done. Did she really have this much work to do or was it her way of keeping him off?

He said: 'I'll iron the shirts. Been doing it all my life.' He fetched the ironing board from the kitchen. His shirts and all the rest of his washing was done at the launderette, but even if he hadn't worked there he thought that he would make his own arrangements for clean underwear. How could you ask a lovely lady to wash your socks? (No man was a hero to his valet.) He fixed up the ironing board and, while the iron warmed, he did the washing up. When he returned, Caroline was writing to her father.

'You should stay in more evenings,' she said, without looking up. She was writing in an armchair, with the pad on her knee.

Bobby licked a finger and touched the iron. 'I'm quite useful, aren't I?' he said. 'Give my regards to your dad. Why don't you invite them up here? It's months since they came.'

This remark, calculated to appease, was, he realised as soon as he had made it, a mistake. Mr and Mrs Ford had visited them once in the two years that they had been married, although Caroline had been down to see them several times. There had been much good-natured chat from Mrs Ford, during her solitary visit to Heatherside Estate, about not coming again until they had a baby to show her. There was a big difference, she said, between in-laws visiting you and grandparents coming to stay. She gave the impression that she would be holding herself in readiness down in Piddletrenthide, Dorchester, for a quick dash up to their place once she had been given the new, more acceptable role.

Caroline, remembering too, didn't answer. Bobby laid a pink Marks and Spencer's shirt face down on the board and began to iron. The silence hung heavily in the room. Caroline, huddled up on the chair now with knees and feet on the cushion, was frowning but writing quickly: it was her trade. He would finish the ironing, produce a bottle of Entre Deux Mers, and corner her on the sofa.

But when he had finished the shirts, and taken them upstairs, the letter was still unfinished and so he opened the wine anyway and sat on the sofa alone.

He sipped the wine sadly and remembered when they had first married and her face had seemed to fill up with pleasure when he said something nice about her. He remembered how she had posed originally—and quite misleadingly—as a lovely scatterbrain, leaving obscure messages about the house, like 'your frilly knickers are in the oven, dear heart.' He had loved all that. What he didn't like at all was all this. Having waited so long to get married, he had given himself plenty of time to paint his own idealised picture of what it was all about and for two years Caroline had preserved it. She did not nag, she never argued about money, she never indulged herself in the angry silence, she was never lazy. She didn't make sarcastic remarks

73

about his men friends nor bitchy ones about other women because there was no rancour in her. She had been a happy housekeeper, an inventive cook, a lovely bedmate and an easy-going companion; and when he came home drunk it was only what she expected a man to do from time to time.

But all this was when she thought that he was going to be the father of her beautiful children.

He poured out a glass of wine for her. He could see that the void between them had been created by their careful skirting of the subject of babies. It would grow until they talked it out.

Finally, Caroline's letter was finished, and she fetched some brown paper to parcel up the book.

'I've poured you some wine,' Bobby said. 'Come and sit down.'

She was inflexible. 'I'll do the parcel first.'

Cutting Sellotape at the table, she eyed him warily.

'You've got that let's-have-a-serious-talk look on your face,' she said. 'That's why you came home early.'

'Very perceptive, beautiful. Just what I had in mind. The parcel's fine. It's a book in there, not the crown jewels. Come here.'

When she joined him, she sat distantly at the other end of the sofa, putting a full yard between them. She fingered her wine glass nervously. Bobby sat sideways to face her, but did not move any nearer.

'I want to know what happened to my happy, sexy wife.'

Caroline stared down into her wine.

'She's still here.'

'Not so happy, though.'

'And not so sexy?'

'And not so sexy. I know you're fed up about the tests. I know how you feel. But we can't go on like this.'

'I know.'

'What are you going to do?'

'I'm not going to do anything.'

'I'm relieved to hear that.'

'Relieved? Why?'

'The last time we discussed it I got the distinct impression that you wanted to find a man.'

There was a delay of four or five seconds before Caroline

74

chose a reply.

'Don't be ridiculous, Bobby.'

'Well, you sort of suggested it.'

'I was upset. That's all.'

'You're still upset. What I want to know is what I can do about it.'

Caroline finished her wine and held out the empty glass. He filled it up.

'I'm adjusting,' she said. 'I'll be all right. I've got to get used to it.'

He watched her face and he didn't believe her.

'Let's go to the theatre on Wednesday, and see that play you wanted to see?'

She nodded. 'That would be nice.'

In the silence, he said: 'I love you.'

There was nothing else to tell her. He looked across at her to emphasise his words. Her eyes had filled up with tears.

'I love you, too,' she said. 'That's the trouble.'

'Bullets don't hurt, you see. Chiefy Morris said to him, "You've been hit, you know." And he looked up at Chiefy Morris and said, "I'm sorry, but you've lost your right arm." Chiefy Morris didn't know.'

On the way with the drink, Bobby tried to work out how this contribution to the conversation from Edward the landlord (who, he now realised, had the Second World War engraved on his face) was linked with the conversation earlier about the barmaid's immense breasts. Even conversation in public houses had a certain logical development about it. He tried to remember what he had half heard, and soon the pieces fell into place: from the barmaid's bosom to Elizabeth Taylor had been a very short step, and from Liz Taylor it had moved on to Grace Kelly when Roland had suggested that Prince Rainier's memoirs would be called *My Heirs and Grace's*. From Princess Grace they had moved to Jacqueline Onassis, and from there to the assassination of President Kennedy and to the effects of bullets on the body. There you go.

The landlord of The Crown wasn't too careful about his pipes: it was keg beer but you could smell the hops. When it was Bobby's round, he switched them all on to whisky. The conversation stopped drifting and lodged firmly on the familiar rock of Roland's frustration.

'I wouldn't mind slipping a length up the mammoth Scandinavian,' he said. 'The nearest I've been to a sexual experience lately is finding lipstick on a café cup.' He downed his whisky in a gulp and bought everyone another, telling the barmaid that she could have whatever she liked from a bitter lemon to a multiple orgasm. The girl smiled, not understanding.

With his new drink, he began to wonder whether he might solve his problem by using a computer-dating organisation. 'You tell them what your favourite colour is and they send you the addresses of six ugly nymphomaniacs,' he said. 'All for twenty quid.'

Bobby had an idea of his own. Half drunk himself, he would get Sinclair so plastered that he would be crawling on all fours. He would get the pig so drunk he couldn't even lie down. He beckoned the Swedish lady and financed a river of whisky. It was Steve Sinclair's round but he was full of memory gaps.

'You'll get me drunk,' said Roland. 'My head's rattling. Heads supposed to rattle?'

'Your nose is never far from a pot of ale,' said Bobby. 'As someone once said about somebody.'

'You said it about me. I just heard you. You put it away yourself, I can't help noticing.'

Bobby shook his head. 'I'm a secret lemonade drinker,' he said.

He bought a packet of cigarettes and tried to remember when he had bought the last packet. Roland hadn't mentioned the sterility problem lately, but he didn't want to discuss it in front of Steve Sinclair. What he would have liked to introduce into the discussion was Lynn Sinclair's *cri de coeur*. So many topics were taboo that it seemed safer to concentrate on the drink. The coupon in the cigarettes said: 'If you do smoke cigarettes leave a long stub. Remove from mouth between puffs. Inhale less. Take fewer puffs.' If you *do* smoke cigarettes? Why did they think he had bought them?

Steve Sinclair, he was glad to see, seemed to be drinking with both hands. Eventually he went to the lavatory.

'I don't think you like him much,' Roland said. 'The hate's coming off you like steam.'

'I never have liked him, even before your party.'

'You're two different types, that's why. You're a man's man and he's a woman's man.'

'I wondered why I couldn't stand him.'

Roland waved a finger. 'No fighting, though, Robert. Fighting is the language of the inarticulate.'

Bobby looked at roly-poly Roland, reaching into several pockets for a cigar, and wanted to tell him that he, at any rate, was all right. Then a fresh thought protruded through the alcoholic haze: was Roland subsidising him. Was the job at Easy Clean, which had enabled him to get married and buy a house, an absurd act of generosity from his fat friend? There was money to spare at the end of the week, he knew that, but with rent and rates on the shop and on the office where idle Della day-dreamed, what was Roland making out of it? Being innumerate he had never wondered before. The harsh columns of the balance sheet were braille to him; men became rich or went bankrupt without any reason that he could see. He had always assumed in a disinterested sort of way that people like Roland, with money, would always survive, but, of course, it wasn't true. Sometimes they went bust.

'I don't want you worrying about money,' he said. 'It doesn't go with your carefree personality. We'll double the take when we open here, and everything will come up fivers.'

Roland looked lugubrious. 'I hope you're right. I'd still like to have a new idea, though. Did I ever tell you about my very first one? I raffled my wage packet.' The memory seemed to fill him with pride. 'I was working in a factory, during school holidays, for about ten pounds a week. I bought a book of raffle tickets for an old sixpence and flogged the tickets all round the factory for two bob. The winner got my wage packet, unopened.'

'And what did you get?'

'Never less than fifteen pounds. Sometimes over twenty.'

While they both admired the ingenuity of adolescent Roland, Steve Sinclair returned looking drunk.

'I ought to eat,' he said. 'Soak up the beer.'

'I'll buy you a pork pie,' said Roland.

'Don't do that. I'm a vegetarian.'

'So was Hitler,' said Bobby.

77

Roland laughed. 'Hey, Steve, do you want to join our gang-bang team? We're playing the barmaid away next Saturday.' He looked at Bobby who was laughing. 'If we *had* a gang-bang team I'd wind up on the substitutes' bench.'

'My God, you blokes can certainly put it back,' Steve Sinclair said. He looked white.

'Have another,' said Bobby, signalling for a Scotch. 'Do you realise there are ten alcoholics in France for every one in England? A lot of people round here aren't pulling their weight. Ten to one, for Christ's sake. We can't even win at bloody drinking.'

Sinclair took the new whisky without much enthusiasm. 'Damaged stomachs, bleeding ulcers, people falling downstairs,' he said.

'What's he on about?' said Bobby.

'The boy's rambling,' said Roland. 'I think he's trying to tell a joke.'

'Laugh? I thought I'd never start.'

'Alcoholism,' Steve Sinclair said, struggling over the pronunciation. 'Terrible business. My uncle died of it.' His face looked more porous than ever.

'No danger of it happening to you, the drinks you buy,' Bobby said.

'Is it my round? Never let it be said.' He stared blankly round the room.

'Cheers,' said Roland.

When they got up to leave they were drunk. Roland tried unsuccessfully to kiss the barmaid. Out in the street, the bright daylight blinded them.

Roland put his arm round Bobby's shoulder. 'Another fine mess you've got me into, Stanley,' he said.

'Oh dear, oh dear, oh dear,' said Steve Sinclair.

'A most comprehensive dissertation of woe, old fruit. Do you want a taxi or a priest?'

'I must go home and sleep it off. Where's my car?'

They went into the car park. Roland tried to get into a Bentley, forgetting that he had a BMW. 'If I get breathalysed now it will be a *Guinness Book of Records* job,' he said.

He eased his new car on to the road. Sinclair, in a white Cortina, followed them cautiously.

'A quiet night in front of the telly this evening, I think,' Roland said, as they left Alford. 'The great thing about telly is you can expose yourself to the most beautiful women and the police can't touch you.'

He pushed a cassette and the Beatles sang *Obladi Oblada*. Behind them, as they came onto the dual-carriageway, Sinclair was striving to keep up.

> *'Mary ran a knocking shop in Basingstoke,*
> *Sally did the best blow job in Brent,'*

sang Roland to the music. 'What comes next? Be inventive.'

'Someone was Miss Handjob up in somewhere,' said Bobby. 'And someone somewhere something something bent.'

A hundred yards behind them as they accelerated away, Steve Sinclair came awake suddenly and was driving at a tree. He hauled the steering wheel round violently to keep his car on the road but succeeded only in putting himself into a lethal four-wheel drift that took the Cortina sideways on to the grass verge at over sixty miles an hour. The car hit the tree with a fearful force and when it had bounced off it and come to rest in some bushes over thirty yards away, Steve Sinclair lay across the front seat like a man in a deep sleep.

Eight hundred yards up the road, the lyrics were complete:

> *Mary ran a knocking shop in Basingstoke,*
> *Sally did the best blow job in Brent,*
> *Maureen was Miss Handjob up in Manchester*
> *Yet their brother was a vicar down in Kent.*

Bobby stared at Tim Franklin's face. Tim Franklin was looking creative. It was a strain being creative. You could tell from Tim Franklin's face. A decision would emerge from the pain eventually; Tim Franklin was giving the strongest possible impression that it would be a decision well worth waiting for.

Bobby stared at the chess board between them. The position looked simple enough: if Tim didn't move his bishop he would lose it. But there were some chess players who refused to recognise the simple: they craved for the complex. Tim Franklin looked like a famous photograph of Boris Spassky in the last days at Reykjavik.

The chess club met every week in one of the many rooms in the art college. All that the club owned were the boards, the pieces, some chess clocks and a pile of score sheets. They were locked away in a filing cabinet and left at the college between meetings. Tonight they were all in use, the boards laid out on card tables with two men at each peering distantly down at the sixty-four squares as they tried to visualise what the position would be in three or four moves if they followed a certain line. It was a game that had always fascinated Bobby. He liked its possibilities and its restrictions. He was never going to demolish a Muhammad Ali, or score six goals in a cup final, but he could not see why he shouldn't find the move that was brilliant, or dream up a combination that would destroy the very best opponent.

Tim Franklin was coming out of a deep trance. He adjusted his horn-rimmed spectacles with his thumb, advanced his queen's pawn, and hit his clock. Bobby wrote the move on his scoresheet and then he wrote his move, too. He took the bishop, hit his clock and went for a walk around the room.

Chess was probably second only to cricket in its classlessness. At the next table a florid bank manager was staring at a coalman's pawn to king four as if he had never encountered it on a chess board before. He clicked a flintless lighter repeatedly before covering the board with a cloud of sweet-smelling pipe smoke. The click of a lighter and the odd cough were all the noise you got in a chess club. Bobby strolled over to another table where one of the youngest members, a boy of ten, was doing terrible things to an accountant. The boy advanced his queen lethally and smiled happily up at Bobby. Bobby winked back.

He didn't like to arrive at the chess club with a hangover like the one that his lunchtime session in The Crown had given him, but he was confident that he could beat Tim Franklin standing on his head with a pint of bitter in both hands. He went over to the notice board and saw that he had been picked to play against Alford in a league match the following Monday, and then he returned to his own game. Tim Franklin, minus bishop, had castled.

Bobby lit a cigarette, looked at the board and then studied

his scoresheet. It said: 1 P–K4, P–KN3; 2 N–KB3, P–Q3; 3 N–QB3, B–N2; 4 B–B4, N– KB3; 5 P–Q3, P–KR3; 6 QB–B4, 0–0; P–K5, N–R4; 8 P–Q4, NxB; 9 0–0.

He was a piece up. How could he lose? He decided to chase Tim Franklin's other bishop away and moved his queen bishop's pawn up one. Tim moved his queen up a square to threaten Bobby's knight. He didn't want to swap it, so he moved it to rook four, and Tim immediately moved his king rook's pawn. Bobby looked at the board for some time. He had only used eleven minutes. Tim's clock showed half an hour. Certain hideous possibilities were beginning to appear. The advance of the king knight's pawn would win Bobby's knight.

'I don't like losing, Timothy,' he said.

Franklin stared at the board. Victory meant a lot to him, too. To vacate an escape square for his knight, Bobby moved his bishop into the corner. Like a rocket, Franklin took the offered pawn with his queen. There were still a few strategems for saving the game, but Bobby was too muzzy to see them. He looked at the white queen looming ominously on his side of the pitch, and decided absentmindedly to resume his hunt for white's other bishop. He moved his queen knight's pawn two places. Tim Franklin ignored the threat and placed his knight next to Bobby's knight. The game was over.

'Want another one?' Tim asked, stopping the clocks.

'Do I buggery,' Bobby said. 'What a ridiculous game. My brain's in neutral.'

The other players were paired off now so there was no point in Tim staying. They left the room and walked down one of the college's long corridors.

'If you look through that door there, you'll get a pleasant surprise,' Tim Franklin said. He was nodding at a door ahead of them and on their right.

'What sort of a surprise?'

'There's a bird in there without clothes on.'

'I like ladies without clothes on,' Bobby said. 'We've all got our weaknesses. How do you know?'

'She's there every Tuesday, modelling for the sex maniacs of the life class.'

Bobby opened the door silently and eased it forward a few inches. Josie was lying on her side on a couch facing the door.

The class of twenty or so extremely mature students had their back to him. Her nudity didn't seem to disturb them as they worked away with their brushes, but it disturbed Bobby and he closed the door not knowing whether she had seen him.

'Do you know her?' he asked.

'Wish I did. If they get her pubic hair right, they'll have to send out for more black paint. I wonder why she poses like that?'

'I think it's very sexy of her. Very kind. Fancy a drink?'

'Okay. I've got a car here somewhere.'

It was a yellow Dutton B which looked as if it might be useful in traffic jams for overtaking buses underneath. Bobby climbed into the tiny passenger seat with difficulty.

As he drove out of the car park, Tim Franklin said: 'Did you hear about Steve Sinclair?'

'What about Steve Sinclair?' The name came back like a cloud.

'Dead.'

'Dead? How?'

'They found him in his car tonight. He had crashed off the road somewhere between here and Alford apparently. I got it on police calls this evening.'

'How did it happen, for God's sake? Did he hit anything?'

'Evidently not. It's a bit of a mystery because it was some time before they found him. His car had gone off the road and was obscured by some hedges. You know what it's like—it's a quiet road out that way. He could have been there hours.'

'You mean he could have been alive after the crash but nobody knew he was there to get an ambulance?'

Franklin shrugged. 'Maybe. I don't know. There'll have to be an inquest.'

But Bobby didn't need to wait for the coroner. He could see Sinclair's Cortina tearing off the road and into the trees while the driver, full of Bobby's whisky, fell asleep over the redundant wheel.

'Christ,' he said. 'Does his wife know?'

'The police will have told her by now. What's she like? I've got to go to see her in the morning.'

'What for?'

'Obituary. Prominent local estate agent. Member of Rotary

82

or Round Table or whatever it is that businessmen join to get away from their wives. She's a bit of a misery, isn't she?'

'I expect she is by now.'

Tim Franklin pulled his car up in the square, and they climbed out. A cold wind blew over them. Bobby's desire for a drink had vanished.

'I won't come in after all,' he said. 'Thanks for the lift.'

Tim locked his car. 'Has that trouncing at the chess board killed your thirst?'

'That's it.'

He walked across to the launderette and locked up and then headed for home, leaning into the wind.

It had been a day of surprises. Losing at chess came as a fresh surprise every time. The death of Steve Sinclair was a massive shock that had left him groping numbly between relief and guilt. And there was another waiting for him when he escaped from the cold into the centrally heated warmth of his home.

Caroline wanted him to make love. The unspoken message could have been written in blown type across the grey wallpaper of all four walls. She was sitting at the table with her typewriter on one side, as she drafted her replies in pencil to the Susan Smith postbag. But she was smiling and relaxed. More importantly, the jeans had been replaced by a skirt. Thighs and other stimuli—a good two inches of cleavage showing exactly where last year's sun tan stopped—were on display. She had always made the message clear to him.

'Hallo darling,' she said. 'Early home two nights running? Did you have a quick win at the chess club?'

'I had a quick defeat at the chess club.'

He slumped in an armchair and wondered how he felt. It didn't require a lot of self examination: he felt awful. It would be tomorrow before he was fully recovered from today's whisky, and Steve Sinclair's death had affected him most peculiarly. It was the last night he would have chosen to restore sexual activity to the family programme. He lit a cigarette and it burned his throat.

'What's new?' he said. He meant: Are you going to tell me about Lynn Sinclair's letter?

83

'Susan Smith has had a rise of £5 a column.'

'She deserves it. Upholding the puritan ethic, waging war on sin. All on her own, too. Anything else?'

'A woman in Reading wants to know if oral sex is illegal.'

'Jesus.'

He half expected her to ask him whether it was. Oral sex was not her favourite activity and they had only tried it twice in two years. But despite the blank spots in her sexual repertoire, he refused to find it even slightly odd that a girl with Caroline's limited experience should be delivering advice professionally on the nation's bedroom problems. She probably thought that zoophilia, coprophilia and urolagnia were the names of newly liberated countries in darkest Africa, but what did it matter? The country had always been badly served by its 'experts' and what an old-fashioned magazine with old-fashioned readers needed were old-fashioned ideas.

'Do you want a coffee?' he asked.

While he was making it, he began to feel angry at his wife's secrecy. It seemed to him that he was entitled to be told about the letter to Susan Smith; it was his business, too. He found a Watney's beer tray that had obviously started life in one pub or another and put the coffee and a plate of biscuits on it. He put the tray on the table where she was working and sat down opposite her. As usual, he was disarmed by her breasts. He wanted to want her and after a while he did. He wanted to bring them together again, bury himself in her body, bury the past. Bury Steve Sinclair.

He said: 'Why didn't you tell me about Lynn Sinclair's letter?'

Caroline looked up. 'How did you know about that?'

'I read it over breakfast. I'm surprised you didn't think it worth mentioning.'

Caroline was unruffled. She took a biscuit.

'Well, I love you going through my mail, darling. Of course I thought you would be interested. But after what happened at Roland's party I thought it would be best if you didn't know. I didn't want you two going at each other again like a couple of punch-drunk boxers, getting fined for assault. He apparently brings out the violence in you.'

Bobby dunked a biscuit in his coffee. Her answer impressed him.

'What are you going to do about the letter?'

'Ignore it. There are over forty of them here and I only need twelve. It's such a stupid letter anyway. What can I possibly say to the woman? What we need are questions that a lot of people would probably ask, problems that are shared by hundreds of other people. You couldn't say that about her letter.'

'But it made you feel good, though.'

Caroline drank her coffee, put the cup down and sighed.

'Bobby, I don't know what's the matter with you. You're getting terribly insecure. I suppose it's the test thing. Steve Sinclair is a nice young man but I would never want anything to do with him. Not like that, anyway. I can't help it if he fancies me. Just forget about it.'

Steve Sinclair was getting dismissed today in a big way.

'It's been a bad few weeks,' he said.

'I know. We had a shock. We've got to get over it. We'll go to bed in a minute and get over it.'

She is wearing her Susan Smith hat tonight, he thought. He loved her but she was a machine. Cool and efficient, sensible and single-minded. She was a long way from yesterday's tears. The transformation in only twenty-four hours was a small miracle. Women were resilient creatures.

He took his coffee and went over to an armchair. A copy of her magazine was lying on a cushion and he picked it up. All women's magazines looked the same to him. On the cover, along with the flawless face that had appeared on a thousand magazine covers, was a list of this week's exciting contents: Clothes To Cut A Dash In; Beautiful Bathrooms; Pregnancy And Drugs; How To Get Your Hair Into Shape; Filling Your Freezer; Win a Caribbean Honeymoon! He turned to the Susan Smith page. It was all words apart from a line drawing of 'Susan Smith' in the top corner, an elderly woman, kindly and understanding, everybody's favourite aunt.

'Steve Sinclair is dead,' he said.

'Pardon?'

'He was killed this afternoon in a car crash.'

'Oh no!'

'Absolutely. He's extremely deceased.' He felt happy for the first time in weeks. Her replies had taken the clouds away.

'I got him drunk at lunchtime and he drove into a stationary tree. Do you know, my first reaction was relief? I know it's awful but it's true. I saw him as a threat even before Lynn Sinclair's letter. I thought, that's got the bastard out of the way.'

Caroline stood up. 'Poor Lynn.'

'Probably not.'

He remembered how aggressive she was, like a kitten who had been badly treated.

'Her life will probably begin now.'

'How did it happen?'

He told her what he knew. 'I feel rather guilty about it,' he said.

'Why should you do that? He's a grown man. If he wants to get drunk that's his business.'

Susan Smith was definitely on form today.

'I did rather push the hooch his way.'

'Why? I thought you hated him?'

'I wanted him to make a fool of himself. I wanted to humiliate him, I suppose. A drunk man is very vulnerable. If he had been arrested for being drunk and disorderly, or drunk and incapable, I'd have regarded it as money well spent.'

'It solves the problem of what to do with Lynn Sinclair's letter.'

Bobby collected the cups. 'Susan Smith doesn't know that Steve Sinclair is dead.'

'Susan Smith knows everything.'

'I want us to go to bed.'

'She knows that, too.'

In the bathroom he felt young again; the nightmare was over and hope had returned. Caroline was fine and Steve Sinclair was no longer menacing his marriage. He took off his clothes and stepped under the shower. It was amazing how the human race reacted to death. A man's life was extinguished, and it seemed to merit no more than ten minutes of conversation before the subject was unanimously changed. He remembered years ago when a friend had been drowned in the Solent. Telling someone about it soon afterwards, he was shocked to find the conversation turned almost immediately to his listener's undramatic experiences at sea. No man's death diminishes me because I don't take any notice of it. Tomorrow, or the day after, he would go round to Mrs Sinclair to see that she was all right. Before he went, he would make up something that Steve had said about her during their visit to The Crown, something loving and gentle that she could remember for the rest of her life. It wouldn't have to be too good, though, or she would never believe it.

He stepped out of the shower re-born. It was like a party in his teens. Waiting for him in a bed in the next room was a lady. Never keep a lady waiting. He only hoped that after all this time he could remember what to do, but there were two things you never forgot and one of them was how to ride a bicycle. He grinned at himself in the mirror, a mutual exchange of congratulations at the way things had turned out. He put out the bathroom light and wrapped a towel round his body to conceal his enthusiasm.

Caroline was lying in bed, listening to the radio news. She turned it off and smiled at him.

'Why are you hugging that wet towel?' she said. 'Are you getting shy in your old age?'

'Didn't want to scare you, lady.'

She pulled the towel away from him. 'You're awfully big tonight, Bobby.'

'The condition is strictly temporary, madam. It won't last more than three or four hours.'

But the day that had been memorable for its surprises had, like a practised scriptwriter, saved its biggest one until the end, for as the purple sheets fell slowly over their naked bodies, expelling the air from inside the bed, his nose, which was always the keenest of his senses, told him unmistakably that somebody had been making love to his wife.

FOUR

Bobby sat at his desk and read the morning paper:

He appeared calm as he knelt before the chopping block.
His hands were tied behind his back but he was not blind-
folded. The executioner, a tall Saudi dressed in yellow robes,
displayed no emotion as he wielded the sword on a dais in the
square outside the city's Palace of Justice.

The watching people cheered and applauded as he slashed
the man's neck three times before the head rolled from the
body. Witnesses said the sword rose and fell at one minute
intervals to increase the suffering of the assassin.

When he finally lay dead, his long white robe splattered
with blood, his head was hoisted briefly on a wooden stake.

Well, that was one way to go, he decided. He listed and
eliminated other unpleasant deaths, not all of them now
available to consumers. After a tight semi-final with the gar-
rotte, the death of a thousand cuts met flaying alive in the
final. The death of a thousand cuts, with slices being lopped
off the body like meat at a butchers, had done well to get this
far in the competition, but it wasn't quite strong enough—too
crude on technique—to take the title from flaying alive in
which they just peeled your skin off, starting, for some reason,
at the knees.

It seemed a suitably macabre start to what promised to be an
agonising day. It was a day for decisions that he was too tired
to make: three hours feigning illness in the bathroom last
night had seen to that.

Sitting at his desk at half past nine, the situation was no
clearer than when he had sat on the bathroom floor chain
smoking at half past two. The problems loomed up, hovered
and then receded like fish in an aquarium. Why hadn't he
told her that he knew? Should he tell her now? Should he
walk out on her? WHO HAD SHE BEEN TO BED WITH?

He slit the mail open with his biro. A rates bill for £112; a letter from a detergent firm saying that their Mr Parks would be dropping in to tell him about their new miracle brand; a letter from the Chamber of Trade urging him to attend their protest meeting about planned rates increases; another notice for his wall, advertising a recital from the local wind ensemble.

What you had to admire, or rather abhor, was the way that she had attempted to lure him into lovemaking so that in the event of a tiny arrival in nine months' time she could try to convince him that he, after all, was a father and the dates confirmed it. Susan Smith had been plotting craftily this week.

He picked up the phone and dialled the bank; it seemed a good moment to establish how the Booth family stood financially. The bank said that they would have a word with the computer and could he call in later? He imagined that he was overdrawn—things were never so bad that they couldn't get worse. He wandered out to have a look at the estate. Two students, statutory record albums under arms, were waiting at one of the spin driers. Four of the washing machines were punishing somebody's dirt but the owners had gone off to do battle in the supermarket while Easy Clean did their work for them.

He knew that there was an important job he had to do around here this morning but there was small chance of his remembering what it was. He had other questions spinning in his head. The one that had pushed its way to the front now—dislodging WHO HAD SHE BEEN TO BED WITH?—was why hadn't he told her that he knew? Why had he shrunk from the confrontation? Why had he ducked it? Cowardice? No. The answer to that, at any rate, was clear: the marriage could hardly have survived if he had thrown it in her face last night.

But the answer to what he should do now was not so easy to find. He didn't even know what he wanted to do. He didn't even know whether he wanted to do anything. He was developing the raddled nerves of a stray cat. Undermined by tiredness, his vision of the world was all gloom: the world was where sick fools threw bombs at innocent people and never told you why; where teenagers maimed themselves by the thousand with drugs or cars; where nice people developed fatal diseases for no apparent reason; and where a few people had a lot of money and a lot of people had no money so that while millions starved a lady in London could spend three million pounds on trying to own a Derby-winning horse. The world—the neurotic thoughts were flooding back from an anguished adolescence—was where friendships faded while fears grew and, contrary to quite normal expectations, each year seemed to be not only shorter but also less interesting than the last.

He stood up quickly to shake off the mood and walked out of the shop to go to the bank. It was market day and the square was crowded with the urban guerrillas of suburbia—choleric clerks, stroppy shop assistants, dissident Rotarians. He wandered among them and felt at home.

The square had once been the market-place and some of the iron rails used back in the nineteen thirties for penning pigs, sheep and other livestock were still there. Today the market survived but the goods had changed. They arrived in large vans which backed up on to the square and opened up to reveal dozens of cheap dresses or shelves of fresh fish. Bobby walked between the stalls that were being erected, stalls that would soon be selling plants and cakes, crockery and handbags, shoes, books, eggs, cheeses, watch-straps and watches. He paused at the bric-à-brac corner—you never knew what you might find —and glanced at two old chiming clocks, some brass candlesticks, a nineteenth-century ink-well, three ugly vases and a couple of ornate ashtrays. There was nothing that he wanted, but there would be buyers here before the stalls came down. The town was the natural capital for a dozen villages in the country, and the people still came in on market day, although whether it was to flush out a bargain or to relive the past, Bobby never knew.

He nodded at Charles II, cast in lead and consigned to an eternity on horseback in the centre of the square. Quite what he was doing there nobody seemed very sure but there was a rumour that he had passed through the town once just before his nine-year continental holiday.

Bobby left the square and crossed the road. People were talking to themselves in the street more these days. Was twentieth-century man cracking up?

The Georgian-faced bank stood next to a tiny shop that specialised in ethnic art, just a few doors along from the Planet.

Inside, solemn girls, with the town's secrets at their disposal, dealt expressionlessly with silent customers. His statement was waiting for him and he sat down in the bank to read it: he could point out their errors then, while he was still there.

During the last year they had deducted £100 from his current account and sent it off to a cathedral appeal, and soon afterwards they had credited him with £44—'per post', according to the statement he received soon afterwards. When he inquired who the anonymous benefactor was, they said that the £44 wasn't his at all. They made it sound as if it had been his fault. The £100, it turned out, should have been taken from the account of a very old gentleman, who had the same surname as Bobby and who was clearly trying to book his seat in heaven.

The bank went on in this way, arbitrarily giving and taking. They blamed the computer and they never apologised.

Today's statement, when he opened it, was a welcome surprise:

		DEBIT	CREDIT	BALANCE
DEC 1	ROLAND HODGSON ENTERPRISES		201	1101C
DEC 2	783856	100		1101C
DEC 10	NATIONWIDE B/S	79		922C
DEC 15	SUNDRIES		250	1172C
DEC 20	783857	50		1122C
JAN 1	ROLAND HODGSON ENTERPRISES		201	1323C
JAN 2	783858	100		1223C
JAN 10	NATIONWIDE B/S	79		1144C
JAN 16	BALANCE CARRIED FORWARD			1144C

He was amazed at how much money they had—the sundries were the cheques that arrived from time to time for Susan Smith. The account had been quietly growing, even in the month that included Christmas.

Perhaps he should take the whole lot out and install it quietly in another bank under only his name before Mrs Booth could get her unfaithful hands on the loot. He put the statement in his pocket and walked out of the bank.

Waiting on the pavement was Josie.

'Good morning, Miss—?'

'Brownlow. Hi.'

'Josie Brownlow. What a lovely name.'

'I came to see you at the shop but you weren't there. Then I saw you heading for the bank.'

'And here we both are. How cosy.'

The yellow T-shirt had disappeared and she was wearing a white blouse with her faded blue denims.

'I'm going to buy you a coffee,' she said.

All distractions were gratefully received. He looked at his watch.

'I always have coffee at coffee-time. Lead on, Miss Brownlow.'

The Cave coffee bar in a corner of the square was where it was at. It was a long narrow room that had been converted into a cave. The walls and the ceiling were an undulating mass of red glass-fibre, with tiny lights buried mysteriously in the cavities of the wall; all that was missing were a few stalactites.

It was here that a new generation, reared on pot and dedicated to the proposition that life was going to be brief but bright, exchanged trendy phrases and small packets—pills, dope—in the smoky gloom, while a juke-box urged them at medium blast to love everybody, selflessly, uninhibitedly, indiscriminately, man. In this environment, Bobby felt old and he cheered himself up with the thought that some of his fellow-coffee-drinkers were going to be sadly embarrassed, socially and financially, if they accidentally reached the balls-aching senility of twenty-eight or twenty-nine.

They slid into some seats in the dark and sat knees to knees over a small table that was embedded in the walls of the cave. Josie stirred her coffee, then remembered that she had put no sugar in and used the wet spoon to scoop some demerara from the bowl. Bobby, noticing, felt an unaccountable tinge of regret.

At the next table a mountain of hair resting on some brown denim stirred in the darkness and at its centre was a face. 'Hi Josie,' it said.

Bobby took a single cigarette from his packet and handed it to her; he had a strong intuition that there might be something irredeemably bourgeois about offering the full packet.

'Is that one of the beautiful people?' he asked.

Josie pouted. She had a round, honest face with a small nose and a long straight mouth that was very good at pouting.

'Don't be old,' she said. 'Don't come on all middle-aged.'

He lit her cigarette with a match. 'I am middle-aged,' he said. 'I've got three grey hairs somewhere. It was only yesterday that I was a teenager, too. It happens very quickly.' He said it jokily, but felt that he was telling her something important.

'Does it make you intolerant of the folk in here? I mean, that's old.'

'Intolerant? Certainly not. Love them. I'm just envious is all.'

He lit his own cigarette. Josie watched him closely, as if she had never seen a man light a cigarette before.

'Tell me about you,' she said. 'The first time I saw you was at the boys' school. It was a hot day and you had your class sitting out on the playing-field. It was that beautiful summer. You were wearing a blue shirt, sleeves rolled up, and sandy coloured trousers, and you were talking about Robert Frost. I thought—I fancy that.'

Bobby was surprised. 'David Frost, more like. You saw me that long ago? How old are you?'

'Twenty. I was eighteen then.'

'Why didn't you come up? I used to be available.'

'Don't put me down. All men are always available.'

'Only for limited duties.'

His reply displeased her. She poked thoughtfully in the ashtray to lose the ash on her cigarette, and then rested her chin on her hand. 'Anyway, the next time I see this fascinating chap he is running a launderette. Funny, I think. And then the other day I was talking to Mr Rossborough and I asked him about you. He told me that you got married and needed more money.'

'How did you come to meet my old headmaster for God's sake?'

'We students mix in academic circles. He's connected with the evening classes. There's a chap of seventy-eight there, taking his O-levels. Mr Rossborough's very keen on that sort of thing. You're never too old to get an earful from Mr Rossborough.'

'That reminds me. I saw you at the evening classes last night when I was at the chess club. I opened a door and there you were. You didn't have any clothes on, did you know that?'

Josie paused. 'Do you disapprove?'

Bobby shook his head. 'I think it's very sexy.'

'Is that what you think? Anyway, Mr Rossborough said that you were the best teacher he ever had. He said you beat your own track.'

'What did he mean?'

'God knows. But he said it was a tragedy you left.'

'It was the money already.' But he remembered the shock on Mr Rossborough's face when he had told him that he was abandoning teaching to work for Easy Clean. He couldn't have looked more surprised if he had found the Pope going through his pockets, but there was pain there too, as if his very best pupil had been caught playing truant.

Josie was carving a valley in the middle of the brown sugar and he studied her face as she played. It was a face, he decided, that would go a lot better on the cover of Caroline's magazines than the series of gaunt bitches who stared offensively from it every week.

'Why is there no such thing as brown sugar lumps?' she asked.

He laughed. The idea seemed delightfully inventive. 'It's something that never ceases to worry me,' he said. 'That and the shortage of blue food.'

He was suddenly aware of a tremendous desire to take her hand and tell her how lovely she was and how he liked her sexiness and her classless voice and the strange, childlike quality of her seriousness; but the darkness of the Cave was full of eyes. He realised with a shock that she was the last woman that he had had. For a few mad moments he toyed with the idea of sliding his hand under the table and exploring her warm thigh. What was there to lose? But he was imprisoned now in his own inhibitions, old before his time, the seed bull with no seed.

The phrase recalled an anecdote. 'Mr Rossborough has a budgerigar,' he told her. 'He calls it Onan. Why do you think that would be?'

Josie refused to be diverted. 'I really don't know why he

calls it whatever he calls it, Bobby. When are you going to tell me about yourself? Where are your parents? Where do you come from? How long are you going to work in a launderette? Why don't you go back to teaching and stop wasting what you have got? Couldn't you stand the hassle?' She added, surprisingly: 'Teaching is a privilege as well as a duty.'

There was a concern in her questions which Bobby recognised. Josie was in love with him.

'My parents are dead,' he said. 'They died within forty-eight hours of each other eight years ago. My father died first, and then my mother. It was one of those old-fashioned love affairs that I was on the outside of. I came down here to teach soon afterwards. Before that I had worked in a hotel, a pub, a café, a factory and a post office. I am one of life's misfits, neither square nor round. There is no hole that I fit. But I'm glad to hear that teaching is a privilege because otherwise, for the money they pay, nobody but a nincompoop would do it. Not that I enjoyed it much. I was probably in the wrong school. The kids I was teaching were ten, eleven and twelve and they had been ruined long before I tried to stick a few interesting facts in their heads. They had no desire to learn. They didn't even have any curiosity. You could look in their eyes and see the CLOSED sign. It's all down to your background and upbringing, innit? Their course was charted from here to the rocks with a Euclidian straight line. Mr Rossborough called his budgerigar Onan because it kept spilling its seed on the ground. Get it?' Unused to talking about himself for so long he finished with a joke.

Josie shook her head.

'My, my. Young people don't read the Bible any more, do they?'

'No, they read Tolkien.'

He picked up his coffee cup but it was empty. Two more voices called 'Hi, Josie' out of the darkness. Across the room a man with straggly hair and a snow-white face said 'Right on' for the tenth time in ten minutes. The juke-box was talking about peace and flowers.

'Can I get you another coffee?' he asked.

She startled him by placing her hand over his. 'Would you like to go to my flat?' she asked. 'And make love?'

95

His heart jumped with surprise. He asked: 'Is there any coffee there?'

She smiled and they stood up quickly. He glanced down obliquely to see whether his rising erection stood out against the tightness of his jeans, and then decided that it didn't matter.

It was cold outside but neither of them noticed. Josie's flat was a living-room-cum-bedroom with a bathroom and tiny kitchen over a new block of offices in the town. It was centrally heated and simply furnished from second-hand shops. He kissed her when she had shut the door.

'You have a profound effect on my profile, Josie.'

'I noticed.'

He went ahead of her into the living-room. Her double bed was in the corner.

'Of course, if you were teaching, you wouldn't have all this time off. You don't seem to do a lot.' She unbuttoned her blouse.

'I open up at seven in the morning and lock up at ten at night. That's a fifteen hour day, seven days a week.'

'A fifteen hour day in the Planet, from what I've seen.'

'Your breasts are amazing.'

'Kiss them.'

He suddenly remember what it was that he should have done in the launderette that morning: change the coin chutes on the machines so that a wash would cost thirty pence instead of twenty. He was keeping inflation waiting.

'I shall probably get the heave-ho for non-diligence.'

'I hope you do. I can't bear to think of you working there. What do you hope to do with your life?'

'I've given up hope for Lent.'

'Why have you still got your clothes on?'

'It is good for a man not to touch a woman. St Paul to the Corinthians. He must be very impressed with me.'

'Lent, St Paul—what is this? Are you turning into a monk?'

She was wearing his favourite Spanish perfume, Tabu. He sat on the bed as she stood before him and buried his face in her pubic hair.

'What do you want me to do?' she asked, opening her legs for him.

Eventually he looked up at her. 'Got any whips and hand-cuffs?'

She laughed. 'You look awfully normal to me. Don't you sleep with your wife or something?'

He took his clothes off quickly. He smelt of Yardley Black Label deodorant—people didn't smell of people any more.

'Show me a normal man and I'll cure him—Jung. Actually, you keep happening along at somewhat tense moments in my domestic life.'

She lay back on the bed. 'Any more quotations you want to get off, or shall we fuck?'

'Your language is brutal, Miss Brownlow.'

'You're just getting old.'

But not too old, he thought, to separate sex from love.

He was on top of her almost desperately, his mouth on her neck, his hands on her bottom. Despite his frustration it seemed to last for ever with new peaks of pleasure following one after the other. Josie had orgasm after orgasm and after-wards lay beneath him bathed in sweat.

'Christ almighty,' she said.

He put his mouth to her ear. 'You *do* read the Bible. I knew it all along.'

She closed her eyes and for a while she seemed to sleep. She turned on her side but hugged the pillow and not him. Bobby got up and wandered round the room. It was a cosy flat. The pictures on the wall had obviously been produced by the burgeoning talent at the art college and he hoped that his opinion of them would not be invited. One of them consisted of three black balls on a white background, the sort of thing that anybody over six could have knocked off in half an hour; another showed a banana and two oranges placed leeringly in phallic juxtaposition. He went out to the bathroom and rinsed his face. A goldfish bowl, filled incongruously with a dozen new bars of soap, stood on a linen basket by the wash basin.

When he returned in self-conscious detumescence Josie was getting dressed.

'That was much better than the launderette floor,' she said.

He dressed as quickly as he had undressed. Josie sat in one of the room's two easy chairs and watched him.

'You haven't asked me why I came to see you this morning?'

she said.

'My charm? My sparkle and wit?'

'No.'

'You wanted to get laid?'

'That was an afterthought.'

'A very beautiful afterthought, Miss Brownlow. You should have afterthoughts more often. They could be your forte.'

'I'm pregnant. At least, I think I am.'

She has been sleeping with somebody else, he thought, and was surprised at the size of his disappointment. He had no sooner found her than he had lost her. He pulled up the zip on his jeans and sat on the bed.

'I'm sorry to hear that,' he said. 'I thought for one glorious moment that you were mine, all mine. You're a very voluptuous lady.'

'Oh, you don't have to worry. I'm quite capable of handling it.'

Bobby started to laugh. 'I *certainly* don't have to worry. I'm just disappointed, that's all. Not that I have any right to be.'

Josie stood up. 'Do you want that coffee?' She looked pale. 'I'll come and watch you make it.'

But when they were in the kitchen her mood changed; tension had replaced the tenderness and the loving girl had vanished. She found some milk in the smallest fridge he had ever seen and took a shining saucepan from a cupboard below the sink.

'Instant, I'm afraid,' she said, busily.

'Lovely.'

He pulled the kitchen's only chair into the middle of the room and sat down facing her. As usual after sex, he felt absurdly happy.

Watching her at the cooker, the truth dawned on him slowly: he had adjusted so completely to his own infertility that he had somehow imagined it to be public knowledge.

'Christ, Josie,' he said, 'I'm sorry to be obtuse. I see now what you are getting at. You think I might be the father. Ah, well. Ah, well, lovely lady. I am not. The reason it didn't occur to me that you thought it is that I'm sterile. Definitely. I've had all the tests. I'm safer than the Pill and I don't clot the blood.'

'How many sugars?'

'One.'

She poured out the coffee.

'Shall we go in the other room?' she said.

When they were in there, she sat at the table in profile to him and stirred her coffee.

'You obviously think I've been getting laid all over the place,' she said. 'It's the normal male out.'

'I don't. I didn't say that. But if you're pregnant—well, certain conclusions do follow. And I'm sterile, honest. I'll show you the papers.'

'Well, I've got news for you. I'm two weeks late which I've never been before, and apart from Christmas Eve at the launderette—when I was tight, by the way—the last time was on a beach at Shanklin in the Isle of Wight in September. With a lifeguard from Bournemouth, if you're interested.' She turned in her seat to face him. 'It's either you or the Holy Ghost. Given your interest in the Bible, I suppose you'll blame him.'

'I must phone my journalist friend, Tim Franklin. If this is the Second Coming he could be into a few bob. They'll probably have to hold the whist drive results over for a week. Holy Ghost Gets Leg Over—it could make the front page in a quiet week.'

He smiled at her but she wouldn't look.

'You don't believe me, do you?' she said.

'Josie, how can I? I'm sterile.'

Suddenly she was shouting. 'You're not sterile, you stupid bastard. Doctors make mistakes all the time. They probably confused the samples or something. Half those quacks don't know what they're doing, anyway.'

His heart was pounding. The world was turning upside down.

But it couldn't be true.

He stood up and walked over to where Josie was sitting and knelt on one knee beside her chair. He looked up into her face, staring into her eyes so that he would see the pupils betray the lie.

'This is too important,' he said. 'I must know the truth, Josie. You must have slept with someone lately.'

She looked down at him, shaking her head sadly.

'Nobody but you since September. Go and see a different doctor and you'll find out for yourself.'

He stood up in a daze.

'You're telling the truth,' he said. 'You're bloody well telling the truth!'

She looked at him, amazed.

'You're crying,' she said. 'What the bloody hell are you crying for?'

Darryl Blundell sat hunched up on a tall stool at the Planet's bar: he looked like a Minotaur. His fleshy fingers were locked firmly round a half-full brandy glass, and he was listening to a eulogy from landlord Basil about his new Sanyo receiver-amplifier as if he were trying to gauge whether one dark night might usefully be devoted to nicking it. Two young girls stood sullenly by his side waiting vainly for his attention.

Bobby came into the bar quickly and ordered a large Bells.

'Shalom,' Darryl said. 'You look as if you've been weeping.'

'Morning Blunders. Cold wind. It's January out there. Are you paying for this? Cheers!'

He drank quickly and sat down. His knees were shaking.

'This is Knickers and Sin,' Darryl said, nodding towards the two girls.

'Hallo Knickers and Sin.'

'Nicole and Cynthia,' said one of the girls tonelessly. She had a white face and long black hair. She and her friend were moodily sipping bitter lemon and Bobby wondered where Darryl had found them.

'How are you Darryl? Got a job?'

'I was a roofing contractor last week. I am now an unemployed roofing contractor. They gave me the boot because of my form. Didn't fancy me too near other people's houses, you see. They thought I'd slip down through the attic and have their Green Shield stamps. How is your lovely wife?'

Walking to the Planet from Josie's flat, excited and confused, he had started to make a list of his wife's possible lovers. It was only a short list but Darryl's name was on it. He was one of the remarkably few men who knew her, he was libidinous and he was out of work and available for afternoon trysts at sexy Heatherside Estate.

Bobby said: 'Going east, the moment at which one crosses the dateline becomes the corresponding moment of the previous day.'

'I thought she looked gorgeous at Roland's party.'

'During his lifetime, a man eats the equivalent of six elephants. Did you know that?'

'And drinks the equivalent of one English Channel if it's you. Don't you want to discuss your wife?'

'Moles tie knots in worms.'

'Well, I don't want to talk about her either. I was just being sociable.'

Roland came in. He had a new brown suit on and a bright red shirt.

'It takes twenty-seven muscles to frown, and fourteen to smile,' Bobby told him.

'He's finally flipped,' Darryl said. 'You could see it coming on.'

'You do look a bit listless, Robert. Gormless, even.'

Bobby nodded. 'No list. Extremely short on gorm. Have an immense Scotch.'

'Jolly civil, old fruit. Bells. I reckon he's been at it, myself. You can always tell with a man. The eyelids drop a little.' He sipped his Scotch and studied the two girls with Darryl.

'This is Sin and Knickers,' Darryl explained.

'Two of my favourite things.'

'We play strip ludo together.'

'Only once,' said the dark-haired girl.

'Only once so far,' said Darryl. 'Do you want to play, Roland? You mark every fourth square.'

'And wind up looking at you in the nude? Not today, old fruit. Here, I'm told that Mr Sinclair went climbing a tree wearing a motor-car.'

'What happened to him?' Darryl asked.

Roland released a small belch. 'Only two point three on the Richter scale, that one. Must try harder.' He turned to Darryl. 'He's dead. Didn't you know? He died hanging on to a piece of opposite lock. Drinking and driving. Never did approve of it.'

'How did you hear?' Bobby asked.

'Everybody's talking about it. They reckon his wife's going

to be loaded. You want to get in there Darryl.'

Bobby noticed that Darryl was taking Roland's joke seriously. Or was he already kept busy by someone else's wife? Perhaps he should take Roland's tip and keep a close watch on his friends' eyelids. He finished ordering the round, forcing Southern Comforts on the taciturn twosome: the bank statement had given him the illusion of wealth.

He attacked his second large whisky and tried to clear his head of problems by imagining Darryl playing strip ludo with the two girls. Strip ludo? It was amazing what went on behind the lace curtains of southern England. If Darryl had any lace curtains on the council estate where he lived with his ageing parents. Still, he could certainly teach the two girls a few things—they could be practised pickpockets by the end of the month. That was how it was with young girls, he thought. One week they were madly in love with a man who was crazy about classical music and before long they were going around with someone who was obsessed with car engines. The poor things struggled to keep up, mastering each new subject as boyfriends changed, but there was this compensation: a promiscuous girl could have a most comprehensive breadth of knowledge by the time she was twenty-one.

However, Darryl's two girls didn't look as if they were ever going to learn anything very much. If the price for enjoying them physically was enduring them socially it looked like a steep bill.

'You're really day-dreaming today,' Roland said. 'I asked if you ever get fed up with your own personality.'

'Sorry. Yes. All the time. Why?'

'You have to change it. It's easy. I was just telling Darryl, whose soul we are trying to reclaim. If you're the sort of person who likes black cars, grey suits, blue biros and white shirts, you've got to get yourself a bright red van, a green biro and a black T-shirt with an animal's face on the front. You become a different sort of person.'

'Without effort you manage to talk fluent cock.'

'But it's true. You beat your own bias. I'm going to have a crew-cut, grow a beard and be circumcised. I reckon that should do the trick for a couple of months.'

But for a change Bobby was not on the pub conversation

wavelength. Having too much to think about had scrambled his mind. Perhaps it was time for a graffiti check. The art students were now back from their Christmas break so the loo should be up to the ballcock with scintillating one-liners. It wasn't. The best of the new entries said: Intercourse is the lazy man's way of masturbating.

He returned to the bar. Roland was saying: 'That's why I've bought this horrible red shirt. I'm going to be a different person. There's something ruthless about a red shirt. Meet the new ruthless Roland.'

'I need something a little more fundamental than a new shirt,' Bobby said, pulling his stool to the bar.

'A head transplant?' Darryl said.

'You buy yourself a mauve denim suit, with black roll-neck shirt and Italian sandals. You'll be amazed how your behaviour actually changes. A jeroboam of Veuve du Vernay for myself, Basil, and a magnum of brown ale for superpleb here. Blimey, this red shirt's working already!'

'It sounds like the same old Roland to me.'

'Listen, I've got my new money idea. Motor-bikes.'

'Motor-bikes?'

'That's it, kid. There's a whole generation that's thirty or forty now that used to tear around on motor-bikes when they were young.'

'I did it myself.'

'Exactly. Well, they can't afford motor-bikes now. They have cars to put their kids in, they've got mortgages. They've got those wife things.'

'So?'

'What they want is a ride on a motor-bike, feel the wind in their hair, if they've still got hair, recapture their lost youth. Roland Hodgson Enterprises is about to accommodate them. Motor-bike hire. Ten pounds a day.'

'If they can buy houses and cars why can't they afford to buy their own miserable motor-bikes?'

'Do you realise that a BMW bike costs two thousand pounds? You can get two cars for that. Anyway, the people we're aiming at don't want to buy one. Their wives wouldn't let them. What they want is the occasional fling. What do you think?'

'I'd have thought ten pounds a day was a bit much.'

'These are going to be very good bikes.'

'I suggest you put an advertisement in Mr Franklin's newspaper before you buy a bike, just to see what the response is.'

'Good thinking, partner.'

Darryl was cleaning his nails with the end of his comb. 'Is the board meeting over? It must be fucking great being a tycoon.'

'You've got to move into the big league, Darryl, old fruit. Why don't you knock off a bank or something?'

Darryl flicked some ash off his trousers. He wore the flamboyant slacks favoured by professional golfers. Today's were a wide check in grey and pink, topped by a black sweater. The final impression was of a moderately successful cat-burglar.

He said: 'I've given up crime.'

'The man has a high mendacity quotient,' said Roland. 'If his lips move he's lying.'

He stood close to the bar as lunchtime trade began to fill the room. Soon he was doing his paraheliotropic act as pretty girls began to appear round the bar.

'I wonder where Heather is,' he said.

'She's left,' said Darryl. 'Gone off with a coach-driver. Ask Basil.'

Roland sighed. 'What a silly woman. I was going to invite her away on holiday.'

'You're not earthy enough,' said Bobby.

'Two weeks in Greece, who cares if you're earthy? Where's the coach-driver taken her? Brighton? What are you doing for holidays this year, Robert? January is the month to book.'

Bobby shrugged. His glass was empty but nobody seemed to be noticing.

Roland turned to Darryl. 'Before this character here went dashing myopically into matrimony, we used to take holidays together.'

'Not sharing the same room, I hope?'

'Oh yes. Very intimate.'

'Do you know that Roland has got a birthmark on his left buttock that is exactly the same shape as South America?' Bobby said. 'You have to go to Malta with him to find out things like that.'

'It's not the same shape. It hasn't got the Falkland Islands at the bottom.'

'It's South America without the Falkland Islands.'

'Anyway, we were in this posh hotel in Italy once, and it had a very strange washbasin that Bobby mistook for the urinal.'

'Roland was so busy washing his feet in the bidet that I thought he wouldn't notice.'

They were all laughing when Lynn Sinclair suddenly appeared. Her face was white.

'Thank you for stopping,' she said. 'Thank you very much for stopping.'

Roland was embarrassed.

'It was great of you two to keep on going when you could have stopped.'

Bobby picked up his empty glass and stared at it, embarrassed too. He found Mrs Sinclair's sentence structure somewhat elliptical.

Roland spoke up. 'I'm very sorry about Steve, Lynn, but I don't know what you're talking about.'

'Oh yes, you do. Racing back from Alford and leaving him there in the wreck. If you'd gone back to help he might have been saved.'

'Lynn, we didn't know he'd crashed. We thought we'd burned him off ...'

'Getting him drunk first,' she said, deaf with anger or grief. 'I suppose it was your idea,' she said, turning to Bobby. 'Just because he fancied your tarty wife.'

Bobby lit a cigarette and said nothing, silenced perhaps by the tiny grains of truth in this crazy spiel.

'Look Lynn,' Roland murmured, putting his hand on her shoulder, 'this isn't doing any good.'

She stood back abruptly. 'Don't touch me, you pig. I just wanted to say thank you, that's all.'

She walked rapidly to the door, spilling a few drinks on the way.

'The vicar fell into the grave and a pall was cast over the whole proceedings,' said Roland. 'It's your round, Darryl. You thought we'd forget in the confusion, didn't you?'

'Who was that nut?' said a man with beer down his shirt.

'Was that Steve Sinclair's wife?' Basil asked, leaning over

the counter.

'No. His widow.'

'I don't think I'll have any more,' said Bobby. The incident had depressed him. 'I've got to change the coin chutes on the machines. A launderette manager's work is never done.'

Roland handed his glass to Darryl. 'Very conscientious, my partner. Bells, no ice, Blundell. Shall we see you tonight, Bobby? If I'm not in bed by midnight I'm going home.'

'Oddly enough, you won't,' he said, remembering. 'I'm going to the theatre with Caroline.'

'The theatre? During opening hours? What do you think matinées are for?'

He went out into the cold wind and left them laughing at the bar. He could see Lynn Sinclair sitting alone on a seat in the square, ignoring the market around her and staring vacantly at Charles II.

The new theatre which had risen on the edge of the town's main car park two years ago, was built austerely like a work-house, as befitted an edifice which owed its existence largely to public subscriptions. Even now, the occasional amateur watchdog could be seen scouting around the foyer, the club-room or the tiny bar, looking for evidence of waste. A dec-ade of wine-and-cheese parties, jumble sales, sponsored walks and summer fêtes had gone into its construction and even with grants on all sides the debt was still not completely paid. With inflation, it probably never would be: the theatre appeal office had a job for life.

Bobby and Caroline arrived as the three-minute bell was calling the faithful, like a muezzin, to their seats.

'You're going to enjoy this play, darling,' Caroline said as he bought a programme.

'Is it the tragedy of two star-crossed lovers in the passionate landscape of Renaissance Italy? Oh no—that was last week.'

'It's about a chap who teaches English. It will fill you with nostalgia.'

'It says here that it's brilliant, sardonic and witty and unsuitable for children.'

'Smashing.'

She was in a remarkably jaunty mood, he thought, after the

débâcle of the night before. The consolation that she would be a lot less jaunty if she heard his latest news was tempered somewhat by the thought that he would probably be considerably subdued himself if he knew hers.

'Lead me to the culture,' he said. 'I think these thespians are a hoot.'

It was a small theatre of 400 seats and most of them were occupied tonight. They found theirs, and Bobby settled down in the darkness to enjoy the abrupt movements, the exaggerated postures and the unexpected vocalities which he always found at the eager heart of repertory theatre. There were no curtains and the scene—an office with two desks facing each other—stood before them, postponing the suspension of belief. More importantly, there was no smoking, although the cast would no doubt chain-smoke throughout.

The play—it emerged slowly—was about a presumably bisexual English tutor at a London university who lurched about the stage like a badly controlled puppet, alienating everyone he met with his vituperative chat: his estranged wife, his ex-boyfriend, his colleagues, his ex-boyfriend's new boyfriend. It was hard to judge it, weighing the actors against the script; an astute playwright might not have let this lot loose on his impacted prose. But Bobby, who went to the theatre seldom, found himself enjoying the lines. He enjoyed the way that the local culture vultures were stunned by two buggers and a fuck in the first half hour, and his enjoyment was greatly enhanced by the fact that the flabby and awkward young man who was attempting to portray the tormented tutor, was, for most of the action, farting helplessly, like a horse after wet oats.

At the interval they went to the bar. Caroline had a Martini, Bobby had a gin. The theatre was the big night out for the town's most notorious attention-seekers and they were here in bulk this evening, he noticed. Finding themselves too many miles from the West End, they raided their wardrobes for the provincial theatre instead, like some crazy nineteenth-century Englishman, dressing immaculately for dinner in the lonely jungle of a distant colony to convince himself that he wasn't missing a thing. The blue-rinsed ladies, with the vivid lipsticked mouths that ageing beauties mistakenly thought fetching, chattered in little groups exchanging malicious confidences while their white-haired husbands stood tamely alongside, defeated by the boredom of the years. A huge poster over the bar revealed that the next production would be a political thriller called *Julius Caesar*.

Mr Rossborough appeared through the crowd, black-suited and bow-tied. With him was the tiny Chinese wife he had acquired during an early teaching contract in Hong Kong. She was wearing a yellow robe that stretched from her chin to the ground, a distance of about four feet. A much-loved staff-room joke during Bobby's teaching career had been that when Mrs Rossborough asked Mr Rossborough what he would like for dinner, he replied: 'One, sixteen and thirty-five.'

He came at them now, all smiles.

'Bobby! How nice to see you!' He smiled at Caroline and waved a finger. 'If I'd known you were going to take him away from me I'd never have introduced you.'

Caroline smiled politely at Mrs Rossborough, and then told her husband: 'It was his choice, Mr Rossborough. But we're glad that you did.'

'Are you ever coming back? The pay's gone up, you know. Good teachers are hard to find. They're all political activists now—Maoists, Trots. Marxist clichés dripping from their beards. I was talking to somebody about you the other day.'

'You said I beat my own track,' Bobby said quickly before Mr Rossborough remembered precisely who he had enjoyed this talk with.

'Did I? Yes. I meant you did things your own way. And a very good way, too. Do you know, the chess club has completely folded up since Bobby left?'

This last news item was directed at Caroline, who took it as a reproach.

'I didn't steal him from you, Mr Rossborough. I just married him. I'm sure that if you made him the right offer he'd come back.'

As usual, Bobby loved the way that his wife stood up for herself against a man who had once addressed him from a very lofty perch.

'Ah, there my hands are tied,' he said, holding up both untied hands. 'Salary scales are laid down, but there *was* a big increase this year.'

Bobby didn't want to teach any more than he wanted to run launderettes, but he nodded at the news as if he was impressed. He was feeling mildly guilty that in two years since he had left the school he had never revisited it.

The bell rang to call them to Act Two.

'Think about it, Bobby,' Mr Rossborough said. His wife smiled a goodbye.

'Who's a blue-eyed boy then?' Caroline said when they were back in their seats.

Bobby didn't answer. The meeting in the bar had set him off for the millionth time on a private search for the job that would suit him. He was wondering what percentage of the population were in jobs that they disliked when the lights in the auditorium dimmed. The second act differed from the first only in that the play's anti-hero ranted more and farted less. The applause was ecstatic.

They walked home under a full moon but they hardly spoke. He wanted to tell her about Josie and that she might be pregnant. He wanted to tell her that it was all right, and that they could have children after all—that the two years without them was just an accident of nature and not even a particularly unusual one. And that it was only a matter of time before she conceived and that relentless sexual activity would be the panacea for this as it was for so many other quite different problems. When she attacked him for his unfaithfulness, he would counter-attack about hers. And then, because they loved each other and because their problem had disappeared, they would kiss and forgive and start again. The scenario was full of holes but he liked it.

The main flaw, he realised as the climactic words were tripping on his tongue, was that Josie might not be pregnant at all, but just the victim of a minor malfunction in the mysterious mechanism of women. Before there could be any gleeful, guilt-shedding distribution of cards on the table, any tearful kissing and making up, he would need to know for certain what was going on within the voluptuous contours of Miss Josie Brownlow. And there was another flaw: perhaps Caroline was now pregnant, by courtesy of Mr X.

Circumspection was what was required tonight: the holocaust would have to wait.

'What have we got for supper?' he asked.

'Supper? You don't eat supper.'

'Well, I've never been sober at half past ten before. Bloody strange feeling. I'm famished.'

They bought some fish and chips at a corner shop on the edge of the town and ate them in front of the television. A thin, earnest young man was asking a wet-lipped priest what colour he thought God was.

The day's events—Josie, the play and its problems, the meeting with Mr Rossborough, the teetotal evening—conspired to put him in reflective mood.

He asked: 'Are you happy, Caroline?'

Caroline fed a chip into her mouth. 'Why shouldn't I be happy?'

'Well, it isn't automatic, is it? God, whatever his colour, doesn't hand it out with the arms and legs.'

'Why? Aren't you happy?'

'I had a friend once who worked in an office. He thought he was happy. One day he ran into the street, crying and foaming at the mouth. The doctors were able to tell him that he wasn't happy at all. Hadn't been happy for years. Funny that. Sort of mistake that anybody could make.' He screwed up the paper that had held his fish and chips.

The thin man on the screen wanted to know what the pressures were that men lived under in the urban situation.

'I'm riotously happy,' Bobby said glumly. 'But what am I for?'

'You can't chase happiness, dear. It's a by-product of doing the right thing.'

'Thank you, Susan Smith. Can you also tell me how anyone can reach my age with so little sense of direction? I'm the rake that never made any progress.'

It occurred to him that in the years when he might have been building a career, he had drifted from job to job; now it was too late to get on the gravy train that carried doctors, solicitors, surveyors, accountants. A man's options diminished annually.

Caroline stood up and stabbed a button at the front of the television set; the thin man's boundless quest for knowledge was reduced to a dot.

The trouble with the launderette job was that it gave him too much time to think. Thinking could be dangerous. Most people never had time to regret the things that they had never done, or the places that they would never see. Man had to be kept busy so that the brain was too pre-occupied with trivia for self-reproach. Abolish work tomorrow and the mental hospitals would be full in a month.

Caroline was yawning. She had heard all this introspective waffle before. 'I'm going to bed,' she said. She went to the door and turned back. 'The curse started today.'

So that was one question answered.

'Well, you didn't expect to become pregnant this month, did you?'

But she had left without answering, and he sat alone for a long time reviewing the undramatic journey of his life.

FIVE

The following morning he was dead. His lungs lacked the flexibility that lungs were supposed to have, and he could feel the fatal patch on one of them that signalled disaster as surely as the red cross painted on the door of an infected house in the Great Plague. Phlebitis had established a beach-head on his left arm, and the headache that was lodged firmly an inch or so in front of his right ear was obviously the trailer for a coming brain haemorrhage. He thought: Jesus wants me for a fucking moonbeam.

For a while he lay in bed and considered the irony. If the great licensee in the sky was about to call last orders on him after yesterday's abstemious, cigarette-free evening, he was an even more perverse old sod than he had always imagined.

He crawled nervously out of bed: he would die with his boots on.

Outside it was foggy. As he walked shakily to work, it shot delightedly up his nose and hit him painfully on his ailing chest. His stomach was in chaos. He felt terrible. When he farted it sounded like lorries colliding.

At his usual shop he rejected the cigarettes that were offered routinely and came out with only his customary salacious newspaper.

He decided to have a chest x-ray; it was always better to know the truth. He opened the shop, put the lights on, and picked the morning's mail off the floor. Then he went to a café a few doors away for breakfast—a cup of coffee—and read his paper until the health clinic opened.

The x-ray department was run by two women. The first gave him one card to fill in about his medical history, and another, telling him that everything was all right, to address to himself. There was also the question of the cost of a stamp. The second lady operated the machine.

'I think it may be too late,' he said, feeling melodramatic. He started to pull off his sweater.

The lady smiled. 'You needn't take it off,' she said. 'Any pens or anything in your shirt pockets?'

He stood against the machine as she placed him.

'And why do you think it's too late?' she said.

'I feel like a four-day-old corpse.'

'That's encouraging. All we usually get in here are hypochondriacs with healthy chests.'

As he was leaving he had an idea. He went up a floor to where Doctor Grimshaw had his office. Doctor Grimshaw was sitting pensively at his desk, waiting for surgery to start.

'I've jumped the queue,' Bobby told him. 'May I have a quick word with you?'

'Of course. But it must be quick. The waiting-room's full.'

Bobby shut the door and went over to Doctor Grimshaw.

'This is extremely confidential.'

'Everything is confidential in here, Mr Booth.'

'Good. Well, you remember all that business of a couple of months ago?'

'The fertility test, do you mean?'

'Yes, that. Well, something rather strange has happened. There's a lady who believes that I've made her pregnant. She's not quite sure that she's pregnant yet, but if she is, it's me. How can that happen? I mean, could there have been a mistake?'

Doctor Grimshaw unhappily rearranged some papers on his desk, and Bobby suddenly remembered, as a curtain rises on a stage, stories about the fallibility of medical practitioners in general and this medical practitioner in particular.

A man once given a clean bill of health by Doctor Grimshaw had dropped dead while hurrying home with the good news; another, given six months to live ten years ago, still opened the batting for the town's cricket eleven. Doctor Grimshaw had once given indigestion tablets to a pregnant woman, treated a malaria victim for flu, and prescribed Codis for a footballer who had broken his neck in a friendly match at Oakway. So far he had not accused a corpse of malingering but on past form it could happen.

'Homer can nod,' he said.

Bobby remembered that the final verdict on his sterility had come from the hospital. The track record there was not encouraging; eighteen months earlier they had amputated the wrong foot of a man who had gangrene.

'Could there have been a mix-up?' he asked. 'At the hospital?'

Doctor Grimshaw explored the edges of one nostril with his thumb.

'There *could* have been,' he said. 'We're talking about human beings.'

'Bugger me,' said Bobby and sat down. 'I've just had a chest x-ray. I expect they'll write to tell me that I've got hammer-toes.'

'Would you like to arrange another test?' Doctor Grimshaw asked. 'To put your mind at rest.'

Bobby stood up. 'There's not much point, is there? Thank you for seeing me, anyway.'

Doctor Grimshaw suddenly looked rather pathetic, sitting alone in his tiny white office surrounded by couches and lights and bottles and equipment that could all get together to mislead him. Bobby shut the door. A bell rang in the waiting-room to tell today's invalids that Doctor Grimshaw's advice was now available.

Darryl Blundell was waiting for him at the launderette. He was leaning against the wall, hands in pockets, by the door to Bobby's office. Two young wives with prams were sitting alongside the spin driers and an old man stood by a washing machine reading the *Sporting Life*.

'Hallo Bobby, how are you?' Darryl said.

'Horrible. How are you?'

'About the same. What's up?'

'Excessive play in the swivels, I think. Got a fag?'

He lit the first one of the day and began to feel better.

'What brings you here? Washing your pants before the next round of strip ludo?' He went into his office and Darryl followed him in.

'I'm one of the jobless. I get bored. It's up to you fortunate people to entertain us.' He sat on the edge of the desk. 'Matter of fact, I'm not exactly over-burdened with the coin of the realm at the moment.'

He took out a cigarette for himself and lit it. He had a heavy puffed look about the eyes that somehow suggested defeat.

'You're finding it hard to make an honest quid?'

'People don't help,' Darryl said. 'They don't give you a chance if they know you've been away. Look at that roofing job. As soon as they knew, I was out. You blokes joke about it in the Planet, but it's not funny.'

'You're one of the walking wounded. I know the feeling.'

Darryl grunted disbelief. 'Life's a piece of piss for blokes like you. You listened when you went to school. I was too busy touching up the girl in the next desk.'

'Well, I'd have touched up the girl in the next desk if there had been one. Instead there was an amazingly spotty boy with BO.'

Darryl just shook his head. 'People like you drift around, get drunk, and money pours into your bank account. I haven't even got a bank account.' He gestured helplessly with his hands as if the world's indifference was more than he could take.

'Darryl, at thirty-two I've got a great future behind me. How

114

much do you want to borrow?'

'I don't know why I stick around in this fetid dump. At least up London you can get a dose off the barmaid.'

Bobby took the mail from his pocket that he had collected on his first visit. Lending Darryl money was obviously a more subtle exercise than he had imagined. The mail was as boring as usual—just three more requests for space on the notice-board: a church needed bell-ringers, a piano-teacher needed pupils, a ploughing match needed paying spectators. Perhaps he should sell the space and get rid of the machines.

A woman at the door said: 'How many washloads can I get in the drier?'

'Three, madam,' Bobby told her. 'See?' he said to Darryl. 'I do work sometimes.'

'Yeah, very exhausting.' He slipped off the desk and paced the room.

'Do you fancy my wife?' Bobby asked him suddenly.

Darryl stopped. 'Why? Does she fancy me?'

He knew that that would be the reply, part of Darryl's constant search for reassurance.

'No idea.'

'She's not my type. Very nice, mind, but too proper for me.'

Bobby felt relieved. Cross that man's name from the list.

'Look, I know you want to borrow some cash,' he said. 'How much do you want?'

'Yeah, well thanks. Could you do me a tenner?'

'I couldn't, but the firm could. Just for a week or so—right?'

He stood up and went over to the safe. The door was open. The safe was empty.

'I've been robbed,' he said, and picked up the phone.

'Robbed? How much?'

'Christ knows.'

He dialled the police station and then opened a drawer in his desk. He pulled out a folder and opened it.

'A hundred and five pounds,' he said.

The money, in notes, was what customers had handed him for change for the machines. The change machines on the walls only turned coins into other denominations.

'Did you leave the safe open?' Darryl asked, pulling the door to look inside.

'I think I must have done.'

A plain-clothes policeman arrived within minutes.

'Drummer, CID,' he said. He was a tall shy man with a very short haircut and a long nose. He looked inside the safe, but didn't touch the door.

'And what's Mr Blundell doing here?' he asked, when he stood up.

'He just dropped in to see me,' Bobby told him.

Mr Drummer took out a blue notebook and wrote something down. He wrote very slowly. Eventually he said: 'We'll get the safe checked for fingerprints, and we'll need yours, Mr Booth, for elimination.'

Darryl remembered something. 'I touched the safe door just now. After we discovered the theft.'

Mr Drummer nodded thoughtfully. 'Quite so,' he said.

'You see?' Darryl said. 'You see what he's thinking?'

'Now if you'll just give me a statement, Mr Booth. When you put the money in the safe and when you found it missing.'

'One of the machines is out of order and you've run out of out-of-order cards,' said a bearded youth at the door.

Bobby found some cards in his desk and took them out to the shop. When he returned the policeman wrote his statement in his little blue book.

'And at what stage did Mr Blundell arrive on the scene?' he asked when Bobby had finished.

'He was waiting for me here when I arrived.'

'What did he want?'

'I came to borrow some money.'

'Quite so,' said Mr Drummer. 'I'll have to ask you to come along to the station, Mr Blundell.'

'That's ridiculous,' said Bobby. 'He wouldn't rob us. He's a friend.'

Mr Drummer put away his notebook and didn't smile.

'I wish I had your faith in human nature,' he said. 'Two and two are four where I come from and if I find one of the few people in this town with a bit of form at the scene of a robbery I'm entitled to draw certain conclusions.'

'You can search me. I haven't got the bloody money.'

The policeman put a confident hand on Darryl's shoulder.

'We'll do that at the station. Not that it'll prove anything.

Don't touch the safe again, Mr Booth. The fingerprint boys will be round in half an hour.'

When they had gone, Bobby phoned Roland's office. Della answered.

'He's seeing someone about insurance and motor-bikes,' she said. 'What will he think of next?'

'Talking about insurance, will you look out the policy that covers this place for theft? Somebody has wandered off into the night with a hundred and five oncers.'

He put the phone down and stood up. Contrary to earlier signs, it was beginning to look as if he might live. He went out and bought some cigarettes, and then set about mending the out-of-order machine. Roland arrived in a panic as he finished.

'How much?' he asked.

They went into the office and Bobby told him what had happened. 'Why would Darryl want a loan if he had just nicked a hundred quid? It's ridiculous.'

'To throw us off the scent,' Roland said. 'I bet that bastard did take it. The police know what they're doing. Do you remember yesterday lunchtime when I said if his lips move he's lying? He was bloody angry with me. I could see that. What a fucking day! My motor-bike scheme has fallen through. The insurance they were going to charge me was ridiculous. I need a drink.'

As they were leaving, the police arrived to check the safe for fingerprints. There were two of them. One carried a small bag. He knelt by the safe and brushed fine dusting powder over the handle.

'The door was open,' Bobby told him. 'They might not have touched the handle.'

'Ah,' said the policeman.

He brushed the powder all over the door.

'There's a few prints here,' he said. He produced some adhesive tape which he stuck carefully on the door and then peeled off. White fingerprints were now on the tape.

'Mr Drummer wants you to give him your prints as soon as possible,' the policeman said.

Walking round to the police station in the cold his breath came out like cigarette smoke to join the fog that had now got thicker. He wondered why Darryl had agreed so easily to go off with Drummer if he had not taken the money. It hadn't assisted his credibility: a few angry protests of innocence were what was required. Perhaps those who repeatedly broke the law took the rough with the smooth: a wrongful arrest one month, a theft that baffled the police the next. The fatalism was depressing.

When he reached the Planet it was full of students. Bobby struggled to find a path through them.

Roland was talking to Tim Franklin, whose long blond hair fell today onto a matching corduroy jacket.

'A very amusing character woke me up at four o'clock to tell me what a good party he had been to,' he was saying. 'So I phoned him up at half past six to tell him what an awful day it was. Hallo Bobby. Have they got the thumb-screws out for Darryl?'

'I didn't see him.'

'He did it, sure as hell. I've been in court on some of his cases. It isn't that he's a villain. It's just that he's so incompetent at it. He blew himself up once trying to rob a gas meter.'

'I heard. I like him. I don't think he did it.'

'Fiver?'

'You're on.'

They shook hands on the bet.

'You can spend some of your winnings now, Tim,' Roland said.

Bobby had a lager and looked at the students. Why did they all have such haggard faces these days? He had never known young people look quite so sick. It couldn't be overwork. Perhaps it was the drugs. A whole generation looked as if it was dying before it had even started.

Looking at his watch he saw that there was only an hour of drinking time left.

'What this hole needs is a club where you can drink when the pubs are shut,' he said. 'In the afternoons, mainly. Think of all the businessmen who'd like to discuss work over a large gin and tonic at three o'clock in the afternoon. Not to mention alcoholics like us.'

Roland slapped him on the shoulder. 'You're a genius! That's it! That's the very idea I've been waiting for. There isn't a drinking club within ten miles of here. Christ, what a beautiful brainwave!'

Bobby had never seen him look so pleased.

'Afternoon drinkers would be big spenders. They take their drinking seriously.'

'You could pick your own barmaid, too.'

'You've won a large Bells in my Idea Of The Year competition. Where would be a good place to open this club?'

'In the town. The customers are on your doorstep and wouldn't have to worry about drinking and driving.'

While Roland was staring distantly into his whisky, his mind at last engaged with a long-awaited money-making plan, Bobby had an even better idea: he would get a second mortgage on his house and go into the club venture with Roland as a genuine partner.

Basil's face loomed over the counter.

'Phone call for you, Bobby.'

The phone in a corner of the bar was an extension of the phone in Basil's kitchen. When Bobby picked it up and said 'Hallo' he heard Basil replace his receiver.

'Drummer here, Mr Booth. We're going to charge Blundell with the theft, but it's not worth a special court. He'll come up on Monday. We're prepared to give him bail if he can find a surety for a hundred pounds and he asked me to ring you.'

'Yes, of course.'

'It's a bit irregular frankly, seeing as how it was you he robbed.'

'Well, it wasn't really. The money belongs to Easy Clean. I'm an employee.'

'Well, if you want to go bail for him will you come round and sign the papers?'

'Okay. On what grounds are you charging him, by the way?'

'He was in the shop before you got back. His fingerprints were on the door.'

'Well, they would be. I saw him open it.'

'Quite so,' said Drummer. 'It's a bit circumstantial at the moment, I know. But it won't be by Monday.'

'Fit him up' is the expression, thought Bobby. He put the phone down.

'They're going to charge Darryl,' he told Roland.

Tim Franklin held out his hand for money.

'Shall we wait until he's found guilty?' Bobby said. 'English justice and all that. I've got to go round the cop shop and go £100 bail for him.'

'You're nuts. You'll lose it if he bunks.'

'Precisely. Look after my beer. And if you're going ahead with the idea of a club, Roland, I want a share.'

'Time you've lent Darryl money, lost your bet with Tim and forfeited £100 bail you won't be able to afford it.'

Bobby signalled a discreet two fingers and left the bar. The idea of a new club had come out of nowhere and he was proud of it. Even better was his later idea to have a share of it. Getting a second mortgage on his house would enable him to go in as an equal partner, something which Roland would presumably welcome if the dismal noises he had been making about his finances were justified.

He reached the police station in a couple of minutes. Inspector Drummer was in the front office.

'You've changed my mind,' he said. 'We're not letting him out yet.'

'Why's that?'

'We want him to make a statement.'

'You mean a confession?'

'A confession would be helpful.'

'He can go just as soon as he has admitted taking the money?'

Inspector Drummer nodded. 'Something like that.'

'And supposing he didn't take it?'

'Leave it to us, Mr Booth, will you?'

He walked slowly back to the Planet. The weather had emptied the streets, but the bar was fuller than ever. The lunchtime drinkers were fighting for space. Buried among them, Tim Franklin was telling a joke. Where two or three are gathered together in my name, one of them will be trying to tell a joke. Bobby looked round for familiar faces among the horde and then realised that Tim's joke was about a sterile husband.

' "I thought artificial insemination was done with bottles," she said, looking for her clothes. "Some do," said the doctor, pulling up his trousers. "But we've got it on draught here." '

'Your beer's getting cold,' said Roland. 'Where's the prisoner?'

'The third degree isn't working. He won't succumb. He won't break down and confess. And they won't let him out until he does.'

'Good thing, too.'

It was just as well that the police had decided to hang on to Darryl, Bobby thought. He would have received the kind of welcome in the Planet that the Japanese High Command reserved for returning Kamikaze pilots. He picked up his lager.

Some delicate flower had ordered Cointreau frappé, and Basil was wrapping ice cubes in a cloth and smashing them with a bottle on the counter.

At his elbow, two businessmen discussed business.

'Wiltshire is very thin,' said the first man.

'You take out Salisbury and Swindon and what's left?' said the other man.

'Oxfordshire is the same principle,' said the first man.

'It's time for a little monosodium glutamate,' said Tim Franklin. 'I'm starving.'

He moved to a corner of the counter where plastic meals were dispensed to the workers. Roland had a different appetite. He was gazing hungrily at a demure secretary who was sipping Babycham in one of the cubicles round the room.

'Sex is all right,' he said. 'But it's not as good as the real thing.'

'She works in the travel agents,' Bobby told him. 'Her name is Cotty.'

'Sounds like one of those awful dolls who wet themselves. Who's the porcine-faced encumbrance?'

'He's the travel agent. She looks a bit flat-chested for your tastes.'

Roland shook his head. 'Not any more. I've decided that what you can't get into your mouth is wasted. Listen, suppose I get some cards printed saying "Will you marry me?" I'd just hand them out in the street to anyone who looked half-way pokeable, then sit at home waiting for the response, which would be massive, of course.'

'When you've got your own club, fatty, they'll come to you.

I'm going to drop in on the building society this afternoon and see what the score is. The way house prices have gone up I should get three thousand out of them easily. How much do we need?'

'Depends what premises we get and what basis we get it on. But if you can raise three thousand, that will be marvellous. Equal partners, catering for the affluent society. "G and T, please Willoughby." Do you think we can find a barman called Willoughby?'

'It's not only that,' said Bobby. 'Once you've got a club licence you can have fruit machines and other little gold mines placed strategically around the room.'

The prospect of limitless wealth hung before them. Roland bought some more whisky on the strength of it. The whisky moved Bobby appreciably nearer to that magic world where money ceased to be important. By the time that Tim Franklin had finished his food substitutes the celebrations had reached noisy dimensions.

'We're going to be rich, Timothy,' Roland told him, with one huge arm round his shoulder. 'But don't worry. We'll still talk to you.'

'You shoot it and I'll shovel it,' Tim Franklin said.

'The way we drink, the place will show a profit even if we're the only customers,' said Bobby.

'I think there's a flaw in that reasoning somewhere, partner, but I've had too many whiskies to put my finger on it.'

'Pity about you being creative, Tim. Consigned to a lifetime of little brown wage envelopes every Friday. You'll never get off the conveyor belt that way.'

Tim shook his head despairingly. 'Yesterday it was motorbikes. Now it's a club. What a couple of drunkards you are!'

'He doesn't believe us,' Roland said. 'He's not capable of grasping the imaginative genius of it all. Ten-ounce brain.'

'Bogged down with whist drives and flower shows. Immersed in obituaries.'

'Amuse yourselves with a little light raillery if you must,' Tim Franklin said. 'I'll see you in the bankruptcy court.'

The celebrations were halted by Basil. Closing time had crept up on them. They went out into the damp fog.

'I don't think people are supposed to live in England during the winter,' Roland said. 'We're supposed to migrate, but nobody told us.'

Bobby left them and made his way back to Easy Clean. The shop was crowded. He went through into his office. There was a large brown envelope on his desk, addressed in childish handwriting to R. Booth. He opened it with his biro. It was full of money. He emptied it on the desk and counted it and then phoned the police station.

'A hundred and five pounds?' said Inspector Drummer. 'Who put it there?'

'I've no idea.'

'Are you having me on?'

'Come round and see for yourself.'

'I bloody well will.'

Bobby put down the phone and stared at the money. Then he looked at the envelope again and realised that he had seen this writing before. He fetched the telephone directory from the windowsill and looked up a number. Then he returned to his desk, sat down, and dialled it. It rang for a long time.

Eventually, a small voice said: 'Hallo?'

'Thank you for returning the money, Lynn,' he said.

There was a silence for several seconds.

'I don't know what you're talking about.'

'You have a most distinctive handwriting.'

'You've never seen my handwriting.'

'Ah, but I have, Lynn. I'm very familiar with your handwriting. But don't worry. I shan't tell anybody. I don't understand why you took it, but thanks for returning it.'

There was an even longer silence on the line now. Then Lynn Sinclair said: 'I just wanted to give you bastards a fright.'

Friday of the following week was the day that he never forgot. Unlike most days—which started badly with the morning melancholy of a hangover, and ended on a happy high of semi-intoxication—it began on a note of unexpected hope and ended in darkness.

He was at the launderette early, as usual.

There were signs that this was developing into one of the less severe winters. A blue sky was fighting the clouds off and the temperature was spring-like.

Sleepily, Bobby helped a little old lady in a cheap plastic mac fold her newly clean sheets. The postman arrived. The day's mail consisted of one self-addressed card which bore the printed message: 'I am pleased to inform you that your recent chest x-ray was satisfactory. A periodic chest x-ray is advised for everyone, however well they feel. Please recommend this service to your friends.'

The news, tersely expressed, rapturously received, gave him such a lift that he needed a cigarette to cope with it. They only killed fifty thousand a year—what sort of odds were those? He inhaled the smoke and coughed. Life was a dangerous business.

The old lady went off gratefully with her luggage; poverty was washing your sheets in a launderette. Bobby turned up the lids of the washing machines to show that they were free. Over each was the message: 'If the red light comes on, raise lid and rearrange clothes.'

He decided that it was time for a leisurely perusal of the latest disasters to afflict the world in general and the economy and the English football team in particular, and went into his office with his newspaper. He was sitting there, feet on desk, when Tim Franklin came in.

'Hallo Timothy,' he said, laying down his paper. 'Come in for a few chess lessons?'

That Monday, playing against Alford, Bobby had won in twenty moves and Tim had resigned after thirty.

He was now pulling a new five pound note from a small brown wage envelope.

'Sorry about the delay,' he said.

It was the Darryl Blundell bet. Bobby had forgotten.

'Where did the money disappear to, by the way? I never heard the end of that story.'

'My mummy told me never to talk to the Press. They'll only put words in your mouth.'

Tim Franklin sat on his desk.

'Why I'm here, apart from to pay your miserable fiver out of my minuscule wage packet, is to find a story. I'm a bit short of news. We published this morning so today we start all over again and it's a bit quiet round here in January.'

'Is that a copy of your journal under your arm?'

'It is. You can have it.' He put the paper on the desk. 'Can you think of any news? I've got to find something today for the early pages.'

Bobby glanced at a headline on the front page of Tim's newspaper: Mystery of Motorist's Death Crash Unsolved.

'By the year 3700,' he said, 'the weight of all the people on earth will equal the weight of the earth itself. It seems pretty worrying to me.'

Tim Franklin scowled. 'I don't think that you understand my job. I deal in local news. What about your mad club idea? I heard that you're actually making progress.'

'We are. We've got the lease on some rooms over the iron-mongers in Church Street. I'm getting two thousand on my house. All we need is a club licence, and the word is it won't be difficult.'

Tim Franklin perked up. 'Great stuff. Just what I need. New Club Planned For Town. What I don't understand is why Roland wants you to go in with him. I thought he was loaded.'

'He is, but he pretends he's not. He hasn't made much money for two years—only what's left from this place when I've been paid—and he's got the rent and rates of this shop and his office. Then there's his mansion, and we're opening up at Alford which will take a lot of capital. He's been spending money like a drunken sailor for two years but he could still afford to do the club on his own. But it was my idea. I insisted on a share.'

'Can I do a story?'

'Check with my partner. We'd prefer publicity just before we open.'

'Push a drink in my direction and you can have some more then. I'll go and find Hodgson.'

Hot on the scent of something new, the news-hound vanished. Bobby picked up his paper. Only two stories received any prominence on the front page. One concerned two school-boys who had set up a new record for the greatest number of miles travelled on British Rail in one week. 'We spent most of the week travelling between Euston and Glasgow because that is the fastest stretch of line in the country,' said one intrepid traveller.

The other story was the death crash. Bobby read every word:

Mystery still surrounds the death of a 25-year-old motorist after the hearing of the evidence at an Alford inquest on Tuesday.

Mr Stephen Gregory Sinclair, an estate agent of Manley House, London Road, was found at the wheel of his crashed car in the early evening of January 15. The vehicle had crashed into a tree, but there was no sign that anybody else had been involved in the accident.

Mr Sinclair was taken to Alford General Hospital but was found to be dead on admission.

Pathologist David Lea said that Mr Sinclair died following severe chest and head injuries. He had also suffered severe brain damage and, at best, recovery would only have been partial.

'It is conceivable that he might have got over his injuries, but only as a cabbage,' he added.

Mr Bob Blair, an estate manager from Acorn Cottage, Oakway, discovered the car which had crashed into a pine tree along the Alford–Oakway road.

He said: 'I caught a glimpse of the car through some bushes and it seemed to be at a strange angle.

'I turned round and went back. I found the person lying in the car.'

He had seen one car far ahead of him as he entered the dual-carriageway at Alford, and two cars passed him going in the opposite direction.

He added: 'While I was by the car I saw three foxes on different occasions cross the road.'

PC Richard Burt, the first policeman on the scene, said: 'I cannot say how the car came to be in that position. I don't know why it should have left the road.'

PC Ralph Thwaites said that he examined the car at the scene of the accident. He estimated that it had struck the tree broadside at about 40 miles an hour. He could see no mechanical reason why the car should have crashed.

In summing up, Coroner Owen Boyd said: 'There is no evidence that any other car was involved, but this does not mean that no other car was actually involved.

'We cannot say exactly what happened. Mr Blair said that he saw foxes on the road. It is a reflex, albeit a dangerous one, that when people find an animal in the road they risk their own lives to avoid it.

'It could have been a fox. He could have fallen asleep. Or it could have been another car. We don't know.'

The jury returned a verdict of accidental death.

OBITUARY: Page 10.

He put the paper in his wastepaper-basket, surprised that there was no mention of alcohol. Perhaps there was an official reluctance to defame the dead. Mystery Of Motorist's Death Crash Unsolved.

He stood up as Josie arrived at the door.

'Hiya,' she said.

'Miss Brownlow! How lovely of you to drop in.' He walked, mock courteous, and kissed her hand. Above her blue jeans today she was wearing a thick green sweater that concealed all her curves. She looked dumpy but the wind had brought a lot of colour to her cheeks.

'Good news or bad news, whichever way you look at it,' she said. 'You're fertile. But definitely.'

'When did you hear?'

'This morning. Pudding club. Got any fags?'

He handed her his packet. 'I can't deny it's very good news for me,' he said. 'But it's going to play old Harry with your modelling caper. Fancy a coffee?'

He lit her cigarette and then lit one for himself.

'It's certainly put you in a jokey frame of mind. But you're quite right. Pregnant nudes aren't quite what they've got in mind.'

They walked through the launderette into the street. Bobby was exhilarated. First the x-ray result and now this. Suddenly, the clouds had gone. Pessimism was dead. He bought them coffee in The Cave, and they found an empty table in a corner. Around them, long-hairs planned revolution over Coca-Cola.

He wondered what he ought to do to comfort her if she was going to be upset: the news had such vast significance for him that it was hard to adjust to the fact that it was a considerable development for her, too.

'I went to see the doctor last week,' he said. 'I asked him if it was possible that they had made a mistake.'

She stirred her coffee idly. 'You weren't going to take my word for it.'

'I was. Really. I believed you in your flat. I just wanted to see how he reacted.'

'And how did he react?'

'He sounded as if mistakes were just something you have to expect in this world.'

'He's right for once.'

He took her hand in his.

'You don't have to worry, Bobby. I'm asking for nothing.'

'What are you going to do?'

She looked absurdly desirable in her clumsy, thick-knit sweater. Her round, honest face was an invitation. He thought: Where were you when I needed you?

'I might have an abortion,' she said. 'I haven't really decided yet. I'll tell you this, though. If you were single I'd drag you up the aisle. I know it's not very fashionable at the moment, but I rather fancy cooking your dinner.'

He stared into his coffee.

'If I was single you wouldn't have to drag me. You're a remarkable lady.'

She took her hand from his and picked up his cigarettes.

'Give us a light, guv.'

'It's bloody ridiculous,' he said, when they were both smoking. 'I spend two years trying to have a kid and now—an abortion? Do you want any money?'

'I have money.' She looked at the name on the cigarettes and asked: 'Why don't you buy decent cigarettes? Your fags are like fresh air.'

'Low tar. Kills you slower. Look, whatever you decide to do, I'd like to help. Financially.'

'Up to you. My dad's loaded. What's your wife like, anyway?'

'Lovely.'

'No doubt. Why does she send you out into the world in such an extreme state of sexual frustration? Risky thing for a wife to do, I'd have thought, with lovely girls like me about.'

He laughed at her and took her hand again. He suddenly saw how sad she was.

'You're right. It was all because of this little crisis we've been going through. The exciting drama of my alleged sterility. But it's all going to be all right now.'

'Great.'

For a moment he thought that she was going to cry.

'I must take you out to dinner one night,' he said. Powerless to help, he wanted to offer her something.

'Only if you throw in breakfast,' she replied. 'Shall we have more coffee with some of this money you want to lob around?'

He took their cups back through the darkness to the counter. 'There's no way I'm not going to finalise it by tomorrow,' a pale, thin young man told his companions at a nearby table. Bobby winced. The new generation not only looked as if it was dying on its feet, it was going to polish off the English language before it went. A girl at another table said: 'Crabs. This big.' It was fun being young.

He took the coffees back to Josie.

'I think I'll write to Susan Smith,' she said. 'Do you ever see her column?'

'Sometimes.'

'She'll say: "You should have kept your knickers on, you silly bitch." She's like that. A very prim lady, Susan Smith. It's her versus the permissive society. I should think that her husband is going potty for it. If she's got a husband.'

Cramped up at the table, which reminded him of his old school desk, he tried to see from her expression whether it was pure chance that Josie was discussing his wife.

'Have you had one before?' he asked.

'A what?'

'An abortion.'

'Oddly enough, no.'

'I thought most girls are on their second by the time they're twenty.'

He had read an article on the subject recently: obscure private clinics, get-rich-quick doctors from the Middle East, tiny limbs in dustbins.

But Josie knew the other side. 'There's nothing to it,' she said dispassionately. 'But it used to be awful before they changed the law. Unfrocked midwives in back street council flats, and straight home with a bottle of castor oil and a pain in the belly. They used a syringe, if you want to know.'

'I'm not sure I do.'

'There are people complaining now about the new law and the number of abortions being carried out. If they knew how many were being carried out before, and the circumstances in which they were being done, they'd shut their ignorant teeth.'

'You sound awfully knowledgeable.'

'We've got three hundred girls at the college in their late teens. We run a special advisory service in the Students' Union.'

'Where will you go?'

'London.'

'And the cost?'

'I'll let you know.'

He put his hand on her arm.

'I'm sorry, Josie, really.'

'Don't be. If you remember, it was almost entirely my fault.'

'I didn't mean that.'

He finished his second coffee with a few gulps. The cups were made of glass, and the coffee looked like washing-up water with lather on top.

'I meant I am sorry that nothing can come of this.'

'Don't be that, either. Life's too short.'

She put out her cigarette. 'I have a lecture at eleven-thirty. What's the time?'

'The big hand's on the five and the little hand's on the eleven.'

She stood up.

'Will you let me know what you decide to do?'

She gave him a very masculine wink.

'Sure as death, baby.'

In the early afternoon he walked out of the shop and into the square. It was showdown time.

He weaved his way through the heavily ladened housewives, busily buying weekend supplies like regimental quarter-masters with a hungry army at their backs, and headed for home. No more drunken debates at midnight: this would be settled in the cold sobriety of the afternoon. He would tell her that the doctors had made a mistake and he would have to tell her about Josie. He might tell her that he knew she had once been unfaithful to him—it depended on how she reacted. It would be easier if he did not have to throw that in her face. There would be less to clear up.

It would be traumatic, of course. It would not be pleasant.

But the trauma and the unpleasantness were necessary hurdles to eventual happiness. It was the only route he had. Like steel tempered by heat, his marriage would come out of it stronger and more resilient. For often in the past he hadn't felt married at all. The whole business had sometimes seemed to him to be a charade in which he imitated real husbands—a loving cliché here, an unexpected kiss there—when in truth he was still a man alone. All that was about to change. There would be a new dedication.

The prospect excited him. He felt revivified.

He strode past the electricity showrooms and the super-market and the porn shop on the corner (lubricous reading-matter and cut-price cigarettes). The January sun looked down approvingly.

Heatherside Estate in the afternoon was something new to him. It was as silent as a doctor's waiting-room. The men were out somewhere, selling their lives to cope with a morass of bills, and, in many cases, the women were out working, too, put back on the treadmill by inflation.

His neighbours were a mixed lot: their only common ground was the monthly mortgage repayment. The surprising thing was that he seldom met any of them.

It was all very English, he thought, as he looked round at the neat box-like houses that surrounded his own, but it had compensations. There was no problem about keeping up with the Joneses. He didn't even know which ones the Joneses were.

A few he knew. In the other half of his semi-detached lived the Derek Fortescues. He was a swarthy, miserable young man, a good six inches shorter than his bird-like wife. He was in public relations, but what he related publicly Bobby had never found out. His wife, who had the nervous, basilisk gaze of a de-ranged seagull, had once told Caroline, during one of those cosy moments of confidence which wives enjoyed when they were borrowing two pounds of sugar, that Derek *needed* her. From what Bobby had seen of Derek's face, which grew longer as the months passed, he needed her like a wrist-watch needs a magnet.

A tenser, more solemn liaison existed in the house directly opposite. The Rupert Grays even made mirthless jokes about the fact that they had married at Hastings and were now repenting at leisure. Occasionally the sound of violence had carried across the lawns between, but everyone was very polite about it. Rupert Gray was a draughtsman but his salary never quite matched his expectations of himself and he took it out on his wife.

Bobby's neighbours on the other side of a driveway that led to both their garages were two of the older residents on what was a predominantly young estate. The Arnold Russells were the eyes and ears of the estate, filling their retirement years with hopeful vigils behind their pink curtains, checking the neighbours' movements and visitors. In the unlikely event of an orgy of wife-swapping breaking out, the Arnold Russells would be the second to know. Small, grey-haired Mr Russell was a man whom Bobby was happy to avoid, but Caroline, trapped permanently at the scene, had politely endured two compulsory tours of his conversational material. It consisted almost exclusively of some excruciatingly boastful anecdotes about his allegedly triumphant past. As he had devoted his juice years to being a small-time haberdasher in Alford, the monologue was strong on pathos.

Both Mr and Mrs Russell were at the window now. Bobby's unexpected arrival in mid-afternoon was obviously the dramatic high point of their day.

He waved to both of them, took out his front door key and began to rehearse a few phrases for Caroline in his head. When he opened the door he could see why his arrival had been of such particular interest to the Russells. His stomach lurched. On the stairs in front of him was a pair of men's shoes, one on the bottom step and one half way up.

He closed the door silently and stood motionless in the hall. Straining to see what he could hear, he heard only the beating of his own heart.

But it couldn't be avoided any more. With a dry mouth,

he crept quietly up the stairs. When he reached the top he could hear the rhythmic creaking of a bed.

The open bedroom door was only six yards away but it seemed to take him a long time to get there.

Bracing himself for a massive shock he was still stunned and sickened by what was waiting for him.

Pumping frantically—desperately—between the spread-eagled thighs that he knew so well were a huge pair of etiolated buttocks on one of which was the purple shape of South America.

He said: 'Hallo, old fruit.'

SIX

He had frightened himself with a vision as a boy and the vision had been absorbed into a recurring nightmare. He would lie in bed at the age of five and say to himself: If I started to travel away from the earth I would never reach anywhere but would go on travelling for ever. There were no brick walls at the edges: the journey continued, through galaxy after galaxy at ten million miles a second, for ever. It wasn't his epic journey that frightened him as he hurtled through space but the total insignificance of planet Earth.

He woke from the nightmare now, millions of light years from another soul, and stretched out his arm in the darkness. The naked bottom that his hand found was unfamiliar to him and he struggled to reach full wakefulness but his eyelids were weighted by the night before. The bed was harder and smaller than his own and there was only one pillow beneath his head. The bottom that his hand was now touching was smaller and silkier than his wife's, and as his hand caressed it, it was pushed nearer to him so that he could explore its contours more thoroughly.

Something had happened, but the familiar symptoms of a

hangover covered his mind like a fog. The air on his face was colder than he was used to in a bedroom and he slipped lower under the sheets. There was a hand on his thigh now and after some time he was able to work out, mathematically, that it could not be his. It was a busy hand that would not keep still even when it had reached its destination. Its delicate manipulations revived him.

Memories returned painfully, but his whereabouts was not among them. Only a large, economy-sized hangover arrived complete with memory gaps. Reclaimed from space, he lay on his back urging his mind to put the pieces together. He found that he felt better if he did not try to open his eyes or move about. The hand that had coaxed him to rigidity was resting between his legs. He reached down to find it. Perhaps he slept. He dreamed that his hand was taken from him and delivered gently but firmly to some warm thighs. Hair brushed his face as a body rolled towards him, but he was gone again as his mind searched for new galaxies in a black world where only the twinkling lights of obscure planets illumined his Odyssey. He awoke in the act of love, a warm body on top of him, working skilfully towards its climax and his. Breathing in his ear quickened and exploded in a gasp. He lay in the limbo between sleep and consciousness as the body slipped away from him.

He woke up in Josie's flat in the late morning. Sunlight filled the room. From a transistor in the kitchen came the sounds of Rimsky-Korsakov's *Scheherazade*, instead of the modish chat of disc-jockeys. Here was one young lady who didn't prefer the sizzle to the steak.

Her face appeared round the door.

'You're awake!'

'Am I?'

'A black coffee for you, I think.'

She disappeared and returned a few moments later with a cup of coffee on a tray.

'How do you feel?'

Bobby sat up in bed and took the tray.

'How the hell did I get here?' he asked.

'You don't remember?'

'Tell me.'

'You arrived plastered at half past eleven and passed out on

134

the floor. I undressed you, and put you to bed.'

'Did I happen to say anything during this charming performance?'

'Yes. You said, "Roland's in bed with my wife." In fact you kept on saying it.'

'How boring of me.'

'Was he?'

'Yes.'

After a pause, Josie said: 'I put you to bed, and you went into a deep sleep. You make love very beautifully when you're asleep, by the way.'

'I thought it was a dream.'

'It was.'

He drank the coffee. His stomach felt surprisingly sound. Josie sat on the end of the bed watching him.

'I'm supervising an exhibition at the college at twelve so I'll have to go in a minute. What are you going to do?'

'Do?' He rubbed his eyes. 'Does anyone know I'm here?'

'I shouldn't think so.'

'I'm not going to do anything. I'll stay here. What time will you be back?'

Josie took his tray. 'You've no idea how welcome you are. I'll be back later this afternoon. There's food in the kitchen if you want it.'

'Never touch it. Wears out the delicate membranes.'

She took the tray out to the kitchen and returned to kiss him.

'Don't get up. Have a rest.'

'I'm not going to get up,' he said.

As the effects of his long sleep lifted, his picture of yesterday began to fill out. It began vividly but faded as the day went on so that he was still unable to remember how he had arrived at Josie's flat.

The thing that he remembered best, the picture that he knew he would never forget, was not what he had seen in his own bedroom—the heaving buttocks and, somewhere beneath them, his wife—but the shoes dropped carelessly on the stairs. It was a picture that would haunt him, but it was also a picture that told a story, if only he knew what it was. Had they reached the bedroom in a rush?

He remembered standing emptily at the door and saying: 'Hallo, old fruit,' but his voice had broken as he said it and he could not trust himself to speak again. A second or two passed before Roland groaned, 'Oh Christ!' but whether this was in answer to Bobby or just part of his normal post-coital chat, Bobby never knew. He was down the stairs and out of the house without realising that he had decided to leave.

He began to walk, his eyes blurred by tears. At first he was on the edge of the town and then he was in the country. Pavements disappeared, hedges replaced walls and mist hung over the meadows. It became colder but he was walking quickly and didn't feel it. He was numbed, but only by Roland's treachery. For many miles, his mind couldn't take it in. There had to be some mistake: he had been had. But the jog-jog-jog of the walk jerked his mind to a kind of clarity.

He had lost his wife. He had lost his job. He had lost, with the club idea, his best chance yet of making money. He had lost the best friend he had. He had lost everything and would have to start again. He lengthened his stride, as if he could somehow separate himself from the débâcle.

Dusk fell as he reached a village. A signpost told him that he had walked eight miles.

In a short, badly lit street there was a village hall next to a tiny church, a post office combined with a grocery store, and a small public house called the Duke of Cambridge, which lit up to open as Bobby drew level with it.

The bitter was cold but he drank it greedily. He took it over to the log fire and let the heat wrap itself around his misery. Caroline had been his demesne, invaded not by enemies but by a friend. He remembered being shocked when Sheik Mujibur Rahman had been slaughtered by his own bodyguards. Whom does a man trust?

At first the hatred built up with the beer. It was directed at Roland. But after a while he shifted the blame to his wife. The treachery was hers, and the worse because she had chosen his closest friend to seal his humiliation. Finally, hardest of all, he blamed himself. What kind of man was it who couldn't keep his own wife? Particularly a wife as stable and conventional as Caroline.

'A cold night,' the landlord said, pulling off the dregs on one of his pumps. He was a red-faced old gentleman who had no doubt had the pub all his life.

'Very cold,' Bobby assured him. Any phrases that he could release without troubling his brain would be useful. If he could keep the conversation on this level it wouldn't even distract his train of thought.

But the landlord, perhaps equally unimpressed by Bobby's repartee, disappeared with a bucket of slops.

It was a cosy one-bar pub, sustained by the meagre business of the villagers. There was a juke-box and a fruit machine but the dart board was the focal point of the room and, probably, of the social life of the village. The beer was stronger than Bobby occasionally drank in town: he guessed that four would have him floating.

He bought another one when the landlord returned, and established himself on a stool at one end of the counter. He started to imagine the panic that had followed his departure from Heatherside Estate.

'That was Bobby, for Christ's sake! He was just standing there!'

'Bobby? I didn't notice—'

'Christ! He was watching us!'

'You said he never came home in the afternoon.'

'He never has.'

'Oh my God! What do I do now?'

'What do *I* do?'

Bobby got out a cigarette and hoped that their discomfort was total. He drank his second pint and bought another. Alcohol, the sovereign remedy, cure for aches and pains, treatment for sadness, antidote to tiredness, the answer to all known ills; antibiotic, prophylactic, stimulant and sedative; panacea and elixir. It tasted beautiful.

Soon he had had four. The village's drinkers began to fill the bar. Only eight miles out of town and their accents were different, broader, lazier. One, Bobby noticed, actually had cow dung on his boots.

He collected the fifth pint and decided that the next drink would be whisky. I'm pissed, therefore I am. Descartes.

What I should have done, he thought, instead of fleeing

from the house in a daze, was disembowel the bastard before he could find his trousers. The law was rightly tolerant of that sort of behaviour if your wife was involved.

A little old lady was telling the landlord that her husband was an *au pair* fiend. Vice among the farming community? Bobby leant nearer to listen, but the accent had deceived him. The man was an open-air fiend.

He finished the pint and ordered the Scotch. Give strong drink to them that are sad. This way for euphoria. Soon he would be throwing tentative smiles at complete strangers, but at least the landlord was beginning to show a cerain respect for either his consumption or his spending power.

A young man with a hard face and tattooes on the backs of each hand was studying the record titles on the juke-box. He was surrounded by some sinister-looking mates, and his arm-pit was draped cosily round the back of the neck of an equally hard-faced girl. When the juke-box didn't work, they kicked it.

Why not? Bobby thought. If the juke-box doesn't work, kick it. A man became less critical as he grew older—until he surrendered to that final reactionary spasm just this side of the grave. The strident mouth of the teenage years was the voice of tolerance before you were out of your twenties. At thirty-two, he lacked the energy to condemn. Kick it again, ugly youth.

After a while, the whisky concentrated his wandering mind on some problems that he had overlooked: he had nowhere to live, nowhere to sleep tonight, and January was too cold for haystacks. It had always been at the back of his mind that if anything disastrous happened to his marriage, he could move into Roland's mansion. Tonight that was not the answer. He tried to confront the problem before it confronted him—at closing time. There was always the floor at Easy Clean, but that was probably where she would look first. Could he afford an hotel?

He came out of his reverie to discover that he was staring at the tattooed juke-box-kicker who was now standing beside him at the counter waiting to be served.

'Know me again?' he asked.

'What?'

The youth moved a foot nearer him.

'I said, know me again? Who do you think you're staring at?'

He was wearing a black leather jacket and sand-coloured jeans. Leaving the lavatory too quickly, too often, to get back to his beer had left a small but obvious stain on the front of them.

Bobby said: 'Young man, you plumb the depths of shallowness.'

This did not seem to be the correct reply. Even detached from his retinue, the youth carried a perceptible air of menace. His left hand was now gripping Bobby's sweater.

'Okay. This is an outside job,' he said.

The landlord spoke. 'Knock it off, master Tony.'

'Keep out of this, William,' said the youth. He pulled on Bobby's sweater. 'You—outside.'

Bobby thought that as an announcement this was considerably less encouraging than, 'Your life-vest is under your seat.'

'Have a drink,' he said. Peace in our time.

The youth made a noise that was meant to imitate a chicken.

Through the haze, Bobby remembered other salient facts about the stuff that he had been consuming all evening, aside from its qualities as panacea and elixir. It heightened the lower brain centres which controlled ideas, but it dulled the higher centres which controlled behaviour. The good idea of giving this misguided yob a knuckle sandwich came quite readily, but was he physically alert enough to deliver it?

The whisky spoke for him. 'If you don't let go, I'll have to take up your invitation,' he said.

'Take him, Tony,' said one of his friends who had now gathered round, rescued from boredom.

'I'll just finish my drink and I'll be right with you,' Bobby said. 'Talk among yourselves.'

He drank the Scotch too quickly and felt it burn. When he stood up he felt lightheaded. He went to leave the bar and realised that they were all going to follow. His mind was racing now as he considered the prospect of facing not one but half a dozen. Anger boiled up at the thought that the world was about to kick him around again.

139

As they reached the door he turned quickly, caught the youth called Tony by the back of his neck in a vice-like right-hand grip, and hit him in the face with the door seventeen times.

That was all he could remember about the previous evening.

It was late in the afternoon when he finally decided to get up. On a dark day in January there were not many better places to be than a warm bed, and there was nowhere for him to go, nothing that had to be done. He could feel the heat leave his body as soon as he stood up and he threw yesterday's clothes on quickly and then waited for the depression to engulf him.

Surprisingly, it didn't arrive. Moving around the room looking for those little clues that flats were supposed to provide about their inhabitants, he found himself suppressing a mood of wild exhilaration. An optimism that he could not explain was sending determinedly cheerful signals from his viscera.

On the tiny wooden mantelpiece that stood over the unlit gas fire he found Josie's passport. Josephine Katharine Brownlow. Distinguishing marks: None. The unsmiling face in the picture not only invited trust, but gave it. He put it down and picked up an old brown photograph of a cat called Wobbles. The cat's name was written in childish handwriting on the back of the picture. Another photograph, inscribed Wobbles and Me, showed Josie at the age of about twelve, in short flowered dress, white socks and sandals, standing in a garden and hugging Wobbles to, quite clearly, the mutual delight of both. But what impressed Bobby about the picture was the garden itself which was vast, meticulously maintained and included, behind Josie and to one side, a large swimming-pool complete with diving-board, and, in the background, a huge Tudor house that looked as if it contained at least twelve bedrooms. He remembered Josie's remark about her father being loaded, and wondered whether this was the Brownlow home.

On a small bookcase hanging from the wall in a corner of the room, eight strangely diverse volumes filled only half a shelf: Scaduto's *Bob Dylan*, Cocteau's *Les Enfants Terribles*,

Gordon Williams' *Walk Don't Walk*, Olive Schreiner's *The Story Of An African Farm*, a Solzhenitsyn, a book of Kipling verse, *The Female Eunuch* and the *Penguin Dictionary Of Surnames*. He picked up the last one and looked up Brownlow, but it wasn't there.

At the other end of the room stood a coffin stool and a neglected Welsh dresser. Both drawers were empty and the cupboard below held only a packet of joss sticks and an empty biscuit tin. The lady in question, he decided, was one of that growing band of young people who could throw all their worldly possessions in one suitcase.

Outside, it was already getting dark. Time for the day to begin. A bath was overdue and he went through and turned it on. He looked into the mirror and examined his widening parting. Did men lose their hair because they washed it less often than women and didn't give the follicles a chance? Of course, baldness didn't appear in eunuchs castrated before puberty but the information had arrived too late to save his quiff. He combed out his parting, dislodging equal quantities of hair and dandruff. He had a deciduous head! Was dandruff terminal?

He filled the washbasin and stuck his head in it feeling hilariously happy. He found a brand-new, inch-wide bump on the top of his head which gave him an idea about how the evening's festivities had ended last night at the Duke of Cambridge. With his hair dripping, he removed his clothes and extracted a new bar of sweet-smelling soap from the goldfish bowl where Josie kept them. When the dandruff had been temporarily subdued, he fetched Josie's transistor radio from the kitchen, placed it on a chair beside the bath and climbed into the water.

He switched on the radio. The world was still going on. An RAF Nimrod reconnaissance aircraft had flown over the disputed Icelandic fishing grounds. Beirut had relapsed into terror. There had been another massacre at Crossmaglen. A weak ridge of high pressure was passing across England. He put a wet hand out of the bath and switched across to 'Sports Report'. A cliché collector was talking urgently down his nose: 'After a day of rapidly fluctuating fortunes during which the lead changed hands no fewer than six times ...' He farted lethargically in the water and tried to count the bubbles.

Presently, Josie returned. She came in brightly and sat on the edge of the bath.

'You look fine,' she said. 'How do you feel?'

'I feel quite at home.'

'I was afraid that you'd have gone.'

'Why would I do that?'

'What *are* you going to do?'

'As I haven't eaten all day I thought I might take you out to dinner.'

'How lovely of you.'

She left the room smiling mysteriously, and he got out of the bath and dried. There were no clean clothes awaiting him and he smelt the armpits of his shirt to see whether it would do. It would have to.

Half an hour later, Josie was transformed: calf-length suede boots, mauve denim two-piece, a yellow polo-neck sweater beneath it and a dazzling gold medallion, showing the scales of her Libra star sign, hanging round her neck.

'You put me to shame,' he said.

'Nonsense, you look edible.'

'Talking about edible, let's eat.'

'I must call at college first. I have to shut up the exhibition.'

She locked the flat and they went downstairs. It seemed odd to Bobby to be making his first appearance outdoors this late in the day. He took her hand firmly.

'What do you study at this art college anyway?' he said. 'What priceless knowledge are they tucking into your lovely nut?'

'Textiles. I weave.'

'And what happens afterwards?'

'Like most art students, I expect I'll find that there is no demand for what I've learned so I'll teach other students so that one day they can teach as well.' She gripped his hand meaningfully. 'But that's not what we want to talk about, is it? What happened yesterday? What are you going to do?'

The questions jarred him. He took his hand from Josie and put both hands in his pockets.

'I don't know,' he said. It didn't seem very satisfactory. He explained: 'I went home in the afternoon to tell my wife that, contrary to medical reports that I received last month, I am not sterile. I found her and Roland—my so-called partner, my so-called best friend—at it on the bed.'

'What did you do?'

'I walked out.'

'Didn't you *say* anything?'

'I believe I said "Hallo." I then went for a long walk in the country, had a few drinks, had a fight and woke up at your place.'

'Quite a day.'

'Not at all average.'

'Were you going to tell your wife about me?'

'How else would I know the doctors had been wrong?'

'Would she have forgiven you?'

'That we'll never know.'

A cold wind blew in their faces as they reached the college. Even on a Saturday evening all the lights were blazing as pet projects were pursued privately over the weekend. In the car park there were more bicycles than cars but what few vehicles there were had been painted garishly: an old Austin was covered in blue and pink stripes, an even older Morris had been given the psychedelic treatment. From the windows of a room upstairs came the cheerful sound of traditional jazz.

The office of the Students' Union was the local branch of Oxfam, the centre of the campaign to restore free milk, the place where you set about sponsoring a child in the Third World, signed petitions for the reform of the drug laws, supported squatting, attacked Apartheid. It occurred to Bobby that while old ladies died after eating cardboard in Lancashire, the philanthropic gaze of a hundred thousand students was focused remorselessly on the requirements of Ulan Bator, Lamu or the *paracaidistas* of Mexico City.

In this office Josie was the queen. Students bustled around her checking arrangements for a dozen different activities— a sponsored walk for Oxfam, a squat in an empty rectory owned by the Church Commissioners at Oakway, a petition for an improvement in student grants—and Bobby waited by the door while she channelled all the surplus energy. Some of the girls were quite beautiful. Bobby thought: If they stopped pussyfooting around and organised a sponsored fuck they could cover Africa with fillet steaks. Posters on the wall demanded that the reader not only Help The Aged, but also Save The Children.

Outside, he said: 'I suppose they need better grants because they keep wearing their shoes out on all those demonstrations?'

Josie laughed. 'No Fascist sentiments in here, please, or two hundred non-violent, peace-loving students will kick your teeth down your throat.'

They walked along a corridor to where the exhibition was being held. A notice on the door announced that it was of oil paintings, abstract icons and sculpture. Only three people were left. They moved slowly from one exhibit to the next.

'Madonna With Beads' was £90, but 'Leda And The Swan' was only £80. This week's bargain offer: 'Still Life With Violin', £35.

'I have to lock up now,' Josie told the lonely culture hunters. They shuffled out reluctantly and bought nothing.

'Is that the end of your duties?' Bobby asked. 'Are you mine, all mine, now?'

She wrapped her arms around him.

'For just as long as you want.'

He wondered if it were true. He was enjoying her company in a way that he could never have imagined but, daunted by her apparent self-sufficiency, he wondered if there were either room or need for him in her life.

He said: 'From now on, don't say anything you don't mean.'

They walked into the town. The fog was back. Cars crawled with headlights on. Bobby headed for a new restaurant that had recently opened in a street off the Square. He took a devious route that did not take them past the Planet.

Josie put her arm round his waist. 'Is your marriage over, do you think?'

'The marriage is over, but the threnody lingers on. Life's a bit like trying to complete the Tour de France when you've got saddle boils.'

'Is that what you think?'

'That's what I know.'

'Come the revolution, we'll all have a Rolls-Royce.'

'Come the revolution, Miss Brownlow, half of us will be

behind bars.'

'Well, as that nice Mr Lenin said, you can't make an omelette without breaking eggs.'

'And as somebody else said when Stalin locked him up, "I can see the broken eggs, comrade, but where's the omelette?" '

They arrived laughing at the Trattoria Capriccio, and were glad to get into the warm. There was a bar at one end where you could sit and drink while you waited for a place. Bobby wanted a small table for two hidden in an alcove in the corner and they drank a sherry until it was free.

He wasn't used to taking out other women and he watched Josie with interest. She was very sure of herself.

'What happened to Wobbles?' he asked.

'Wobbles is fine. Didn't you think that she's sweet?'

'Tremendous. Where does she live?'

'She lives with my parents in Sussex, near Gatwick.'

'Tell me about them.'

'Daddy's fifty-two. Votes Liberal. Runs a business. Mummy's forty-two. Political allegiance unknown. Doesn't run a business.'

'Runs a very big house by the look of it.'

'Isn't it beautiful? What else can I tell you about my family? During the war, Daddy was a prisoner of the Russians? Isn't that interesting?'

Bobby drank his sherry. Daddy in the war? It was the *déjà vu* show. He offered Josie a cigarette.

'The Russians? Whose side was he on, for God's sake?'

'King George's. He was flying Typhoons when he was twenty. They were the ones with rockets under the wings for blowing up trains and tanks. He was shot down over France on his twenty-second birthday.'

Bobby found it difficult to believe that today's twenty-year-olds could blow up tanks or bridges in France. From what he had seen of them in the Cave coffee bar, they would be stretched catching a bus.

He said: 'By the Russians?'

'No, by the Germans. The Russians were in Russia. He was in a prisoner-of-war camp until 1945 when he was liberated by Russian women.'

'In Russia?'

'No, the Russians were in Germany by then. These Russian women were driving tanks, would you believe? But—this is the funny bit—the Russians just took all the prisoners, mostly British and American pilots, and put them in another prison camp for six months.'

'Why?'

'I don't know. I think they wanted them to fly for the Russians. In the end, a lot of the Americans were shot. That was at Luckenwald in 1945. Luckily it didn't put him off planes.'

'Why luckily?'

'He owns an airline.'

'Jesus!'

She adopted a comic Jewish accent: 'Any time you want a cheap flight, my boy, I'll see you right.'

A waiter appeared to tell them that their table was ready. They took their drinks over to it. As the waiters were Italian or Spanish, and the customers were English, the menu was written in French. Josie ate snails while Bobby had onion soup, and then she ordered fresh river trout seethed in butter and smothered in toasted almonds. Bobby asked for a rare steak. 'Just throw it quickly past a hot fire,' he told the waiter. He ordered a bottle of Petits Crus de France. The traditional affinities of food and wine were of no interest to him.

'What's Roland like?' Josie asked while they waited for the food.

'He's been a very good friend to me for years.'

'With friends like that, who needs—'

'It's amazing. It really is. My wife and Roland. A most unlikely pairing. She's very old-fashioned, sexually.'

'She probably reads Susan Smith.'

'As a matter of fact, she writes it.'

'Really?'

He poured out some wine and told Josie about Caroline's journalism. The truth didn't matter any more.

'So what are you going to do?'

'I don't know. I could always drop out and grow macrobiotic vegetables in Norfolk. It beats working for a pension you'll never live to collect.'

146

'I meant about your wife.'

'Sell her? One careful owner. I don't know what I'm going to do. It's not a day for decisions. Did you know you'd got translucent eyes?'

The waiter arrived with their order. The steak was huge.

'Another bottle of wine,' Bobby told him. The one on the table was still half full.

He said: 'I don't know her any more. I'd have bet my left leg that she'd never be unfaithful. Perhaps I'm just a rotten judge of people.'

He finished off the first bottle of wine as the second arrived. A man at the table outside their alcove was making more noise eating strawberries than most people do eating toast. Bobby scowled at him.

'She must have wanted a baby an awful lot,' Josie said. 'Do you think she'd like mine?'

'She's probably got one coming by now. How is our baby, by the way?'

'Doesn't say a lot yet.'

'Reticent. It's a good fault.'

When he had finished his steak, he ordered cheese and biscuits and a third bottle of wine. He was drinking it like beer. Josie asked for trifle.

'Live it up,' said Bobby. 'This is how the homeless and jobless should live.'

'Let me pay the bill. I'd forgotten that you're out of work, too.'

'A gentleman pays for dinner. The lady pays for breakfast. An ancient tradition which I've just invented.'

'And what would the gentleman like for breakfast tomorrow?'

Bobby drank some more wine.

'Alka-Seltzer, fried. I can't abide them poached.'

Josie played with the bangle round her neck, wondering, perhaps, what their relationship now was. She had done her hair differently, he noticed, so that it was swept back from her forehead to fall down her shoulders. Even in January, when people usually looked their worst, she exuded good health. He wondered how she would look when the sun came.

He beckoned to the waiter and asked for the bill.

'It's been paid, sir,' he said, waving an arm at a distant table. 'The gentleman over there in a green jacket . . .'

Bobby turned in his seat and saw Darryl Blundell eating with the Nicole girl.

'It's nice to have friends,' Josie said.

'Isn't it?'

When they got up to leave, he stopped at Darryl's table. Josie waited for him at the door.

'That was very kind,' he said.

'Think nothing of it. Who's *that*?'

'A friend.'

'Enough to make you whack off all over the ceiling.'

'I'm glad you approve. Thanks, Darryl. Good night, Knickers.'

Outside they headed straight for the flat.

'I must have a bath,' Josie said. 'Will you wash me?'

'What a good idea.'

'All of me, I mean. No cheating. You're not allowed to concentrate on certain parts.'

'Thorough is my middle name.'

The serious Sunday newspapers were aping their more popular rivals. Was Mozart Murdered? 'I am convinced that I have been poisoned,' he told his wife, Constanze. Know the feeling, Wolfgang, you poor paranoic old sod.

Josie's method of dealing with the problem of Sunday mornings was more brutal than Bobby would have liked. For years, the Sunday papers and a packet of cigarettes had delivered him safely to the lunch table, but Josie's tastes ran to long walks, lungsful of cold air, brisk exercise. They walked.

In the park beside the deserted tennis courts the Sunday morning footballers were reliving their schooldays. On a carpet of golden leaves, twenty men chased a leather ball. Their urgent shouts filled the silent world of Sunday for no man could get the ball without receiving a torrent of shrieked advice from his team mates; at this level, all footballers were experts. Boots pounded through the mud, legs soared into the air at impossible angles, bodies collided and lay bruised among the leaves. A man stood on the touchline holding a yellow bucket and a pain reliever spray. Occasionally, he would run onto the pitch very quickly to tend a wounded hero.

They watched the game for some time. A few of the players Bobby recognised as being former pupils of his. Football had been their only interest at school and it was probably their only interest now. Perhaps it always would be.

On the other side of the park, where it sloped away from the town, a queue waited at the par three golf course. Around the perimeter, men in brightly coloured vests were running. That was what was sad about Sundays. It was the day that you saw what people really wanted to do. Tomorrow the demands of the world would take them away for another six days.

The ball rolled over them and Bobby kicked it back.

'I can see you've played this game before,' Josie said.

'In my youth, Miss Brownlow. I get knackered playing chess, these days.'

'I must play you at chess some time. You're good at it, aren't you?'

'I'll play you left-handed.'

They strolled round the edge of the pitch.

'How about a round of golf?' she suggested.

Bobby found the idea vaguely shocking. The girl looked unhealthily healthy, and the sedentary life clearly had no appeal for her. If he wasn't extra watchful, she would try to wean him off the slow pint and the reflective fag and introduce him to the life-enhancing delights of grass-skiing, shark-fishing, orienteering or yoga. A man could grow old quickly that way.

But before he could tell her gently that a round of golf was not his idea of fun, a tiny Oriental lady approached them, closely followed by Mr Rossborough.

'Good morning,' he shouted. 'I didn't realise that you two knew each other.'

'Oh yes,' said Bobby cheerily. He knew that Mr Rossborough would find no scandal in their being together. To him, the world was full of children looking for innocent fun.

'I came over to watch Fitzgerald,' he said, nodding at the football match. 'He's developed into a tremendous striker.'

'He wasn't bad when he was at school,' Bobby said.

'A London first division team is after him, you know. He

could become our most celebrated old boy.'

'He's very strong,' Mrs Rossborough said. 'Very strong.'

As if to confirm this judgment, Fitzgerald, a big, blond youth, took the ball off a player in front of them, swerved past two others and hit the ball into the back of the net from only a few yards inside the half way line. It was a brilliant shot and they all applauded.

'You get great satisfaction when you see a pupil of yours do something like that,' Mr Rossborough said. 'I can remember when he didn't know which foot to hit the ball with. You're missing all that sort of thing in the launderette, Bobby. How is it, by the way?'

'It isn't, as a matter of fact. I've left. I'm one of the un-employed at the moment.'

Mr Rossborough turned to him with a large smile. 'Well, that *is* good news, if you see what I mean.'

'It probably depends which angle you're looking at it from.'

'What are you going to do?'

'I don't know yet.'

He put his hand on Josie's shoulder. He had nothing to hide. Josie relaxed under his touch. He used to find out whether girls fancied him by putting his hand on their shoulder: if they tensed up he knew that he had lost.

'Well, you can come and see me any time, Bobby. The offer's still open.'

'I might take you up on it.'

The Rossboroughs smiled and wandered off down the touch-line.

'That's enough fresh air for one day,' Bobby said. 'What's for lunch?'

'Roast beef, Yorkshire pudding.'

'Not bad, Miss Brownlow. Lead me to it.'

'Will you go back to teaching?'

'I may have to.'

'Think of it—twenty-five-hour week, twelve weeks holiday a year. Loads of laughs.'

'Laughs is what there weren't many of. The only real laugh I had all the time I was teaching was when I under-measured the hundred-yard course for sports day. It got a time of eight point nine seconds for the winner, and there was polite applause from the parents. This poor little bastard had just shattered the world record and all he got was polite applause.'

Josie sat him down with the Sunday papers. Was Mozart Murdered? She would get the Sunday lunch herself. The fresh air had quelled his craving for nicotine. His need was for food. Thick slices of red roast beef appeared with crisp Yorkshire pudding. During her long absence from the flat yesterday, Josie had done plenty of shopping. He was on the pineapple and cream when there was a firm knock on the door.

'That's funny,' Josie said. 'I absolutely never get any visitors.'

She left the table and went out of the room. The next thing Bobby heard was Roland's voice.

'I'm looking for Bobby Booth, whom I believe you know?' he said. He sounded so strained and formal that it could have been somebody else. 'Is he here, by any chance?'

'Yes, he is.'

'May I see him?'

'No.'

Bobby nodded approvingly at the unequivocal response.

'Well, will you ask him if he'll see me? My name's—'

'No,' Josie said. 'He's mine. Go away.'

There was a silence of several seconds. Bobby expected to hear the door shut. Then Roland spoke again.

'I don't know anything about that. It's none of my business. But I must have a talk with him today. Please tell him that. I'll be in the—no, better not make it the Planet. Tell him I'll be in the Square at eight o'clock.'

'Good-bye,' Josie said, and shut the door.

'That was Roland?'

'It was.'

'What'll you do?'

'Do? The world keeps demanding decisions of me. I suppose I'll have to go to see him.'

'I don't want you to.'

'I think I should.'

'You won't come back.' He didn't answer, and she added: 'I know you won't.'

At eight o'clock the Square was empty. There was no quieter

moment in the week. No cars cruised round the one-way system and even the church bells had stopped their unheeded call. Only the leaves, picked up and spun by a trapped wind, broke the evening's silence.

Bobby walked slowly across the red paving stones and then saw that Roland was already there, hunched up in a sheepskin coat on the seat by Charles II. He was staring into the ground some feet ahead of him, his hands plunged deep in his pockets, and he didn't look up when Bobby sat down on the end of the same seat.

'You must go to see Caroline,' he said immediately. 'We've turned this town upside down looking for you.'

'How did you find me?'

'You've been seen.'

Bobby got out his cigarettes and lit one.

'What do you want to see me about? Make it quick. It's freezing out here.'

'I told you. You must go and see Caroline. She's distraught.'

'She'll get over it. People do. Make me an offer for her.'

Roland shifted in his seat to face Bobby.

'You'll have to forgive her. I don't expect you to forgive me, but you must forgive her. You loved her. I know that.'

'It's all destroyed.' He added, to make it clear: 'It's all over.'

Roland made a snorting noise. 'Don't be bloody old fashioned. Throwing the wife out for adultery went out with fly buttons.'

'I'm not throwing her out. I'm throwing me out.'

Roland didn't answer. A priest hurried across the empty square from his empty church.

Bobby said: 'I can't trust her. I can't live with someone I can't trust. It was the first time she has been to bed with someone else. Still, you probably know that. Super-ram in a sheepskin coat.'

Roland ignored the jibe. 'It was only twice. The afternoon we got drunk at Alford. I was plastered. The funny thing is that I sort of thought I was doing you a favour.'

'Thanks.'

'If she'd become pregnant—'

'So you went round yesterday when you were sober to do

me another favour. There's no limit to your kindness, is there?'

'Bobby, I'm not here to defend myself. I promised Caroline that I'd find you.'

'Well, I've got nothing to say to her or you. I'm leaving the shop, by the way. In fact, I've left.'

'Oh, for Christ's sake! Don't throw it all away—the new launderette, the club. We've got it made.'

Bobby thought about it. The beacons at the pedestrian crossing blinked on and off, one always a split second ahead of the other.

'One door shuts and another one opens,' he said. 'You can have Caroline and I shall have Josie.'

'That's the bird I spoke to this afternoon?'

'That's her.'

'Well, all I know is that Caroline loves you and wants you back.'

Bobby flicked his cigarette end at Charles II. She shows her love in a remarkable fashion, he thought.

'You know an awful lot, Roland, but you don't know quite enough.'

'What don't I know?'

'That I'm not sterile. That Josie and I are expecting a baby.'

Roland explored these news items from all angles. It was several moments before their real significance reached him.

'You hypocritical bastard,' he said quietly. 'You must have been knocking her off before I ever went to bed with Caroline.'

'Only once. I was raped. She's a very demanding girl.'

A silence settled round them. Bobby found another cigarette. A lonely car went past. Beyond it, three bored youngsters in leather jackets patrolled the street looking for trouble.

Roland contemplated the ruins of his diplomatic mission.

'I can't blame you for feeling like this,' he said. 'But it wasn't Caroline's fault. It really wasn't.'

'She implored you not to touch her? Don't make me laugh. You were her big hope. Fertile Fatso. She wanted a baby so much it wasn't even natural.'

'I never imagined you could be so bitter.'

'I'm surprisingly unbitter. Just don't give me that guff about it not being her fault. The day will come when I shall be grateful to you. I'm already looking forward to my second marriage.

Of course, I'll have to name you in the divorce, but I won't screw you for any money. But the least you can do is marry Caroline.'

'She's waiting for you in the Planet.'

'In the Planet?' He looked over his shoulder to the pub but could see no faces at the window. 'She doesn't even like the Planet.'

'I brought her. I told her that I was meeting you here at eight.'

'You'd better get back to her, then. But I ought to tell you that the Planet is not the kind of joint she cares to frequent. She prefers classier bars, not that she's all that crazy on bars at all.'

'So I gather.'

'I'm glad you're finding out about her. It could be the start of something big.'

'And you're going to marry Josie? She'll eat you for breakfast.'

'If the red light comes on, raise lid and redistribute clothes. The red light has come on in my life. Time to do a little rearranging.'

'You're incredible. It only seems the other day that I was trying to talk you out of getting married the first time. Now you're all set to do it again and drag me in with you.'

'Time you tried it.'

Roland leaned back in his seat and stared up at Charles II. The mood had changed.

'You don't get to be a bachelor at my age entirely by accident,' he said. 'My allegiance has always been to men rather than women. I don't trust women. I don't even like them half the time. I've wanted them, all right, but I've never let my balls rule my brain. I regard women as the enemy, here to stop men's fun. They're the most lethal minority group in the country. Give them half a chance and they use men, exploit their needs, nag them into submission, wear them out, outlive them, inherit their money. No man was ever as treacherous as the average woman—you've only got to listen to one talking about another. I've been telling you this for years but you haven't been listening.'

'Treacherous!' Bobby said.

'You're entitled to say that, but it doesn't alter the general truth of what I'm saying. If our friendship were to break up over a woman, I'd find it particularly depressing.'

'You're amazing, Roland.'

'Aren't I? Listen, I was in the wrong. I admit it. Caroline was in the wrong. She'll admit it. You were in the wrong. You've made this girl pregnant when you've got a wife at home. But will you admit it? Oh, no! Everybody has sinned except Bobby.'

'You've sinned against me. I haven't sinned against you. Of course it affects our friendship. You've been fucking my wife. What do you expect me to do—give you two sweets out of the tin?'

Somewhere a clock chimed eight-fifteen. A door opened and shut.

'I expect you to forgive Caroline.'

'For a woman-hater, you're awfully solicitous about her. I find that quite encouraging. A crack in the misogynist's façade, perhaps?'

'She's a wonderful girl. I've always said that.'

'A lovely girl. You'll get on well. Of course, if you don't give her a baby a bit quick you'll have to dig her out from under the milkman, but as you keep telling me, that's how it is these days. Women rule.'

'Very bloody funny,' Caroline said, behind them.

They both turned. She was wearing a yellow coat of simulated fur that stopped just short of her knees. Her face was white.

'My first wife,' Bobby said. 'I believe you've met.'

'I'm afraid he's very bitter,' Roland told her.

Caroline stood in silence. The milkman remark had produced the wrong mood in her at the wrong moment and now she hovered uncertainly between attack and defence. Bobby looked round at her but she would not meet his eyes.

He said: 'To save us all freezing to death, I ought to tell you that I have nothing more to say.'

'Where have you been?'

Her voice was firm, Bobby decided. Tears were not on the agenda.

'You have got something to say, though,' Roland said. 'You

ought to tell her. She's not the only one round here who need feel guilty.'

The wind picked up a handbill and blew it to Bobby's feet.

'He's not sterile. He's got a pregnant girlfriend.'

'I don't believe it,' Caroline said quietly. 'I don't believe it.'

'It's true, though,' Bobby said, turning in his seat to face her. 'I was coming home yesterday afternoon to tell you about it but you were otherwise engaged.'

'Why? Why another girl?'

'It just happened. I wasn't exactly creeping out of our house sexually exhausted every morning, was I? You don't mind us discussing our affairs in front of you, I hope, Roland? You might learn something. This is all part of matrimony's rich pattern.'

'I'll leave you two, if you like.'

'Oh, no. Don't do that.'

'I'll do the leaving,' Caroline said. 'I've heard enough.'

' "I've heard enough"! She's been reading her women's magazines again.'

But she was already ten yards away from them and walking quickly across the Square.

He didn't feel the cold now, but sat wrapped in the memory of a three-year-old day when a beautiful journalist had walked into his dreary classroom and made his leaden heart leap. She was vanishing from his life as he watched and yet he felt no pain. What agonies of remorse would ambush him in a week, in a month, in a year? What would he have to live with? He shivered.

She disappeared round the telephone box at the corner of the Square. Two young lovers were making their own connections in the kiosk's warmth.

'Christ, I'm sorry, Bobby,' Roland said.

'Go with her.'

'Do you mind?'

'It doesn't matter any more. The last twenty-four hours have been a revelation to me. Perhaps I married the wrong girl.'

'All husbands say that, at one time or another.'

'But I'm uniquely placed to do something about it, thanks to you. The funny thing is that you are the only person I ever really trusted.'

Roland stood up slowly.

'You should never trust anyone when there's a woman involved,' he said.

Bobby looked up at him. 'Misogynist to the last.'

Stiffly, Roland offered his hand. Bobby looked at it, taken by surprise. The cold pressed in on them.

Then he stood up, too, and, for the first time, they shook hands.

Josie had been crying. He pretended not to notice. When she opened the door to him she looked at him as if he had been dead for several days and was not therefore expected to call tonight. He kissed her on the nose and went past her into the room. She had been sitting by the gas fire drawing doodles with a black felt-tip pen in a small sketchbook.

'Where's the supper?' he said. 'We can't eat out every night.'

'What happened?' she asked, taking both his hands. 'Sit down and tell me. Was he there?'

'They both were.'

'Blimey! What happened?'

She made him sit on the bed while he told her what had taken place in the Square. The change in her face delighted him. Her red-rimmed eyes were wide with hope.

'Golly!' she said when he had finished. '*Now* I'll get our supper.'

She disappeared into the kitchen and he went over to the fire to thaw. He picked up her pad of doodles; they were painstakingly done. He turned the page to see if there were more and found a letter. It had no name at the top:

You were quite right to return to your wife [he read] and I don't want you to have any feelings of guilt on my behalf. I realise that I have brought this on myself quite shamelessly, but I think I can handle it. 'It' includes the baby which I shall have in the autumn and name Bobby no matter what sex it is. You needn't worry about the bills as I come into quite a bit of money in September when I am twenty-one. The only request that I have to make is that we don't see each other any

The note ended there, interrupted perhaps by his unexpected return. He put the pad down and called: 'I like your doodles.'

Her head appeared at the door. 'Doodles? Them is free-form rococo curlicues. Come out here and help me prepare this nosh. Or are you one of those men who believe that a woman's place is at the stove?'

He went into the kitchen and watched her busy efficiency. A beautiful smell was drifting up from a huge saucepan on the cooker.

'A woman's place is in the wrong,' he said.

'I'm not sure I like the sound of that.'

'Women rule.'

'That's better.'

'They do, though, in a most curious way.'

'They fight to rule. But they get awfully neurotic if they succeed.'

'So do the men, but thanks for the tip.'

She handed him a table cloth and some cutlery.

'Give us a hand, guv.'

'There seems to be some mistake. I've been back five minutes and you've still got your clothes on.'

'Eat first,' she said, reaching across him for some floral-patterned plates. 'I don't want you running out of energy.'

He went into the living-room and laid the table. She has a point there, he thought. Energy is what I am going to need large portions of.

Josie called: 'Will we get married when your divorce is through?'

'Yes, please.'

'That's settled then. Let's open some wine.'

He returned to the kitchen and removed the cork from a litre of red. He poured a drink for each of them and they touched glasses, very solemnly.

'May Allah bless us with many camels,' Josie said, laughing suddenly.

'And goats.'

He watched her dish up the food and wondered how he would cope with her capricious vitality. He felt old. Soon every birthday would bring a telegram from the Queen. He took his drink over to the window and looked out. It had started to rain again and the dark, empty street was glistening beneath orange street-lamps. Occasionally the wind lifted the rain and drove it against the windows and then it subsided and was quiet. This was the low ebb of the year. He hated January, the winter, the rain. But in eight short weeks it would be spring again and the sun would be back overhead, drying the damp surfaces of this foggy island and turning them green. Spring was a beginning. Today was a beginning. He remembered the words on the poster at Roland's Christmas party. Today was the first day in the rest of his life.

THE END